Telling Stories Volume 4

Clare Boylan
Stephen Amidon
James Hamilton-Paterson
Allan Massie
Susan Johnson
Roy Heath
Christopher Hope
David Hartnett
Tom Drury
Jane Gardam
Joanna Trollope
E. Annie Proulx
Michèle Roberts
D.J. Taylor
Frederic Raphael
Janice Galloway
Geoff Nicholson
Philip Hensher
Helen Simpson
Robert Cremins

D1344007

SCEPTRE

Also edited by Duncan Minshull

TELLING STORIES Volume 1
TELLING STORIES Volume 2
TELLING STORIES Volume 3

Telling Stories Volume 4

Edited by DUNCAN MINSHULL

SCEPTRE

Introduction and compilation copyright © 1995 Duncan Minshull
For the copyright on individual stories, see page 200.

First published in 1995 by Hodder and Stoughton
A division of Hodder Headline PLC

A Sceptre Paperback Original

The right of the contributors to be identified as the Authors of this
Work has been asserted by them in accordance with the Copyright,
Designs and Patents Act 1988.

10 9 8 7 6 5 4 3 2 1

All rights reserved. No part of this publication may be reproduced,
stored in a retrieval systems, or transmitted in any means without
the prior written permission of the publisher, nor otherwise
circulated in any form of binding or cover other than that in which
it is published and without similar condition being imposed on the
subsequent purchaser.

All characters in this publication are fictitious and any resemblance
to real persons, living or dead, is purely coincidental.

British Library Cataloguing in Publication Data

Telling Stories. – Vol.4:Best of BBC
Radio's Recent Short Fiction
I. Minshull, Duncan
823.01080914 [FS]

ISBN 0-340-62480-9

Typeset by Hewer Text Composition Services, Edinburgh
Printed and bound in Great Britain by
Cox and Wyman Ltd, Reading, Berkshire.

Hodder and Stoughton
A Division of Hodder Headline PLC
338 Euston Road
London NW1 3BH

CONTENTS ∫

INTRODUCTION ∫

A fourth volume, and twenty stories that were broadcast in the last year now take on a second life in print. Our selection was made from the two networks that continue to promote short fiction: Radio 4's *Short Story* programme and the space reserved for readings between evening concerts on Radio 3. Again the collection is a showcase for fresh work with the following appearing for the first time in book form.

Variety is also an aim. Almost impossible not to be electic when over two hundred and fifty stories are commissioned or bought annually. Glance down the list of contents to find writers like Joanna Trollope, E. Annie Proulx, Roy Heath and James Hamilton-Paterson all together, and all markedly different. Customary room is also reserved for a number of emerging voices; this time it includes Susan Johnson, David Hartnett and Robert Cremins.

And there is a mix of preoccupations, too. Far and wide. An impulse to write about things that aren't necessarily on the doorstep. We have been to Czechoslovakia, Hong Kong, backwoods America and the Alps courtesy of precise, vivid tales all under three thousand words in length. The listener has encountered comic funerals, missed cup finals and middle-aged oil-men. And then there was a woman in search of perfect architecture.

But if you missed these and other such imaginative

excursions on air, then now is the chance to catch up with them more permanently on the page.

Good reading!

Duncan Minshull
Chief Producer, Readings,
BBC Radio

Poor Old Man

Clare Boylan

Clare Boylan is the author of four novels and two books of stories. Her recent work includes a collection of writers on writing, THE AGONY AND THE EGO, and THE LITERARY COMPANION TO CATS. She has recently completed a third book of short stories.

POOR OLD MAN was read by Gillian Bevan, and broadcast on Radio 4.

∫

Poor Old Man

A shower of blossom fell on the girl's hair as she looked up. He saw her blue eyes diluted by the light. An arc of satisfaction was laid across her face. Her mouth was open as if to accept a drink.

He prepared a small portion of conversation as carefully as one might set a tray for an invalid. 'Wahlenbergia Hederacia!' he uttered. 'Forgive me, an old man's excitement. It's quite rare.' He was a neat old man defended against the spring in a suit and overcoat. She saw nothing at first, although she looked where he pointed, but when he poked among the sinking cherry blossoms with his stick she crouched down in the grass, and the earth was starred with blue just as the sky was blurred with pink. She smiled at him and he congratulated himself. He had made time and he had lured her into this nest.

The next time she saw him she tried to avoid him. He had talked a great deal on their first meeting, of music and letters and the despoliation of the countryside, while she stiffened in the tree's shadowy roots. When she tried to stand up his face fell. 'I'm boring you,' he challenged. She denied this politely but a corner of his mouth curled ruefully to accept an insult. 'Tell me to shut my trap,' he said. 'It's not often I have the luxury of female company. Since my wife died . . .' He fell silent and spanked the earth with his stick.

She was a young married woman with no ambition. She liked spending the evenings with her husband. Every day she took a walk alone in the park. It wasn't really a park. The land behind a derelict house had a garden run wild and some woodland. Not many people used it and she thought of it as her own place. Occasionally one crossed paths with silent joggers or doggy women, clad in sheepskins or bands of small boys scuttling like insects.

She saw him beating down one of the pathways with his stiff, jointless walk and his puzzled face pulled about by the air, like an old blind dog, and she swiftly aimed her gaze at some other view. But she couldn't help looking back. He was askew with disappointment. He had no cover for this treacherous exposure and he had to suffer her discovery of him more than ever like an old dog; his jaw dropped and his features a map of anguish. She waved and waited for him and he bounded up the hilly walk like a crabbed boy: 'I've ruined your walk.'

'He's an intelligent old man,' she told her husband. 'Sometimes he's quite interesting.' Although they did not meet every day, she got the feeling when they happened upon one another that he had been waiting for her. She told Ben how he rehearsed his speeches in order to have some new piece of information to interest her. 'Sounds harmless enough,' her husband said.

She said nothing. Beneath the inoffensive guise of his old man's body she could feel the iron strength of his will and a force of pride for which modesty was a mask. It was mad, of course, but she felt under siege. In some way, he wanted to conquer her. Her husband thought she was definitely mad.

'If you don't want to talk to him, tell him you prefer being on your own, or walk at a different time every day.' 'He's lonely,' she told him. 'His wife is dead.'

'Poor old man,' he said with indifference.

'What is your name?' He asked her. 'I don't know your name.'

'Angie.'

'Angie, Angie, Angie,' he said.

She had heard the term a new lease of life, but until now had not known its meaning. It wasn't that her old gentleman had shed a decade, but the quotient of life in his ancient bones had soared. His diffidence was gone. He pranced. 'Angel! I shall call you Angel. My good angel!' He reached for her hand. 'My angel of mercy.'

One day when she reached the park he was standing outside. He was looking at the ground and his face was bitter with frustration. She thought of a child put to stand in the playground. Poor old man. Someone had hurt his feelings. 'You're late,' he said coldly. She was so surprised that she laughed.

'I know that I am an old man and of no importance to anyone but I am not used to being kept waiting for an hour.'

'I'm sorry,' she said. 'I had no idea you waited for me.'

He forgave her at once, before she had time to say that she would prefer him not to imagine such an arrangement. His arm linked hers like a clamp. 'There is something else I have to say to you. You did not tell me you were married.'

'How do you know now?' She vowed that she would alter her walk. It was a pity, because she liked walking in the same place, made different by the weather or the seasons.

'I found out from someone else. Your name came up and then someone mentioned your husband. They said you were a devoted couple.'

'I don't like talking about myself,' Angie said.

'No.' He let go of her to turn around and look at her. 'That is your appeal.' He smiled his bitter smile. 'I'm just an old man. When a man's wife dies he knows what it is to be unwanted. Go home to your husband.'

'I haven't had my walk yet,' she said, automatically curbing her stride to adjust to his pace. He picked a wild rose, lividly blushing at its centre and creamy at its hem, with little glossy, fanged leaves. He hectored her with Latin terms before forcing it into her buttonhole. 'A rose for a rose,' he said, and she felt his sharp old fingers raking down her breast.

'You look pale,' her husband said. 'You ought to get out more.' A month had passed and she had not returned to the park.

'It gets a bit crowded in the summer,' she told him.

'Go in the evening.'

She smiled at him gratefully. She loved the way Ben didn't make a fuss. They liked one another exactly as they were and trusted each other completely. 'I won't be long.' She put on a light jacket and went out into the dusk.

The park was different at night. The light went off and the scents came on. She leaned against a tree and felt the damp air, drenched in musk and herb and the heavy fruitiness of rose. She knew every inch of path and had no trouble finding her way.

'You shouldn't be out on your own at night.' A voice rose above the creak of branches. Something hit her on the leg and she gasped. Two small chips, like icicles, had materialised in a stick of darkness which looked like a little, enduring winter tree. 'It's dangerous,' the old man said. With each statement, he spanked her, not too lightly, on the legs with his stick. 'You young women have no sense.' His walking aid seemed to have an eye of its own and rapped out a spiteful, unerring braille as she tried to step out of its way, snapping at branches and tripping on hillocks. 'No sense whatever!'

'I'm fine,' she soothed. 'You gave me a fright. I think I'll go home.' He was right, she thought as she lay in bed. She could still feel the affront in her shins. Young women had no sense. Why else had she run like mad as soon as he was out of sight? Why else had her heart still pounded even after she was safe at home?

After that she went to the pictures in the afternoon. It wasn't as nice as walking but there was the same pleasant sense of solitude. Occasionally she had to move as someone tried to be familiar with her, but she was relieved to see that other men were easily discouraged.

One Sunday in autumn her husband bundled her up in scarves and led her out to see the trees changing colour. He was concerned about her. She hadn't told him about her visits to the cinema and he worried that she was growing dull. He was glad to see her hair blown about, her complexion buffed by wind and air, to hear her laughter as he walked fast, with an arm around her, making her run to keep up.

'Ah, the happy couple!' The stick described a rainbow in the air as the old man emerged from a scribble of trees. 'I've heard a great deal about you.' He thrust a complicated hand at Ben. 'Not from her of course!' A wry grimace for Angie.

'I've heard about you,' Ben grinned at the old man.

'No need to tell me. Boring old fart! I daresay she enlisted your aid on ways to get rid of me.'

'Oh, now,' Ben protested. 'She said you were very interesting.'

The old man beamed at Angie. 'You've got a very nice husband. I can see why you might be devoted.'

Angie touched Ben's hand. 'I am.'

'I said you *might* be!' He waggled his stick at her playfully. 'I'm not so sure.'

'She's quiet but she's deep,' Ben was amused by the game.

'She's deep all right,' said the old man, and he fell silent.

Ben saw that Angie looked uneasy. He put an arm around her: 'We shouldn't tease her. She's a sensitive soul.'

The old man whacked the earth so violently that it caused an explosion of dirt and pebbles.

'I have never teased anyone in my life.' The stick reared up at Angie. 'You've been keeping secrets from me.'

'She doesn't have to tell you anything,' Ben said.

'Who was that man I saw you with?'

'What man?' Angie said.

'I scarcely have to describe him to you. You were gazing at him in such a way as to suggest . . .' He turned aside and his jaw worked fastidiously, as if he did not like the taste of the words in his mouth. 'Tall young man with a hat. Good-looking fellow.'

'That's ridiculous,' Angie said.

Ben looked at her in mild, good-humoured enquiry.

'They came out of a cinema, wrapped around each other. She was eating him with her eyes,' he said to Ben. 'So much so that when I passed her by, she would not give me the time of day.'

'I never saw you there,' Angie said to the old man.

'Where?' Ben asked her.

'The truth, now,' the old man said. 'Out with it!' He spanked her once again with his stick, lightly this time.

'The Adelphi.'

The old man smiled sourly at them. He lifted his hat. 'I bid you good day.'

He thought the join of their hands, which had made them look like a single unit as he spied on their approach, now gave the clumsy impression of something broken and then poorly mended.

'You don't go walking any more.'

'That business,' he said, 'is over and done with.'

'It's good for you,' she coaxed.

The old man gave her a hostile look. 'Good for you, you mean. I bore you.'

His wife ignored this. 'What about that girl you were so kind to – that young widow? She'll miss you.'

'I suited her purpose for a time. She has no further use of me.' He turned away to hide his smile but his wife could only see forsakenness in the stubborn curve of his back, like the carapace of a beetle. 'Poor old man,' she thought.

Scary Movies

Stephen Amidon

Stephen Amidon has written a collection of stories, SUB-DIVISION, and two novels, SPLITTING THE ATOM and THIRST. His third novel, THE PRIMITIVE is published this spring. His work has also been published in the United States, Holland and Poland. Born in America, he now lives in London with his English wife and two children.

SCARY MOVIES was broadcast on Radio 4 and read by the author.

$$\int$$

Scary Movies

I was nine years old when I discovered the Roxy Theatre and learned something about fear. It was 1968, a banner year for fear, with bad news appearing on television almost as regularly as weather bulletins. Every night seemed to bring fresh images of horror and violence. Vietnam, race riots, assassinations, angry protests by long-haired kids not all that much older than me. I'd watch them with my tutting parents, wondering if the world would go crazy before I even reached my teens.

It was on a rainy Saturday in March of that year that my best friend Kevin Bright and I first went to the Roxy. Kevin's mother had gone into the hospital to have what she referred to as her 'plumbing' fixed and so we were left in the care of Mr Bright, an office supply salesman who decided that we should spend the day accompanying him on his rounds. By late morning we'd had enough with being cooped up in the back of his sedan and demanded to be released. So he dropped us off at a movie theatre in a remote precinct of our city's small downtown. To our delight, a triple feature of horror flicks was playing, concluding with *Them*!, the greatest of all mutant ant movies.

The moment we entered the Roxy's lobby, with its thick pillars, oceanic carpet and chandelier the size of a pickup truck, we could tell this was like no movie house we'd ever seen. After a few moments of wonderment we approached the vast concession counter, which was attended by an aged, chocolate-coloured man dressed in a brocaded vest and crisply seamed pants. His eyes smiled at us as we marvelled at the gleaming soft drink fountain, with its brass handles cast like the claws of jungle cats. After settling on some Goobers and Grape Nehi we entered the cinema itself. The film had already started so we stumbled and groped our way to the front row. It was a werewolf movie whose title I have long since forgotten. What I will never forget, though, was the moment when Kevin touched my arm and gestured for me to look at the rest of the crowd. I turned to be confronted by a sea of five hundred black faces. Kevin and I were the only white people at the Roxy.

Now, what you have to understand here is that although we lived just a few miles from New York City, our town was as segregated as any Deep South hamlet. There were two distinct neighourhoods, divided by a downtown shopping district. Our western half was affluent and white, while the eastern section was poor and black. There was little contact between us. True, our cleaning ladies and school janitors were black, though they were a largely invisible presence in our lives. We knew nothing about our black neighbours other than the cruel jokes our parents sometimes told and the occasional spasms of anger we'd see on the local news. To make matters worse, our youthful lore was full of stories about unsuspecting classmates who'd been beaten and threatened when they wandered too far from our safe suburbs.

And so, trapped at the Roxy, Kevin and I sat in stunned

silence and growing dread. Flight seemed impossible. To walk out the way we came in would have meant revealing our Caucasian selves for all to see. Surely we would be taunted, maybe even beaten. It was a good five minutes before I began to hatch a plan that involved a mad sprint toward the nearest emergency exit. But then, before I could say anything to Kevin, the werewolf made his first appearance, leaping out from some dark corner to grasp the heroine's alabaster throat. And with his arrival the crowd, well, the only way I can express it is to say they erupted. In an instant, five hundred kids were on their feet, screaming warnings to the oblivious victim or encouragement to her attacker. Groups of young girls clutched one another in terror; little kids made for the safety of the lobby; some older boys moved fearlessly toward the screen, ready to do battle.

And then, just as quickly as it had begun, the eruption was over. The werewolf was gone and everyone was returning to their seats, chatting and laughing. Kevin and I looked at each other in amazement. We'd never seen kids behave like this before, at least not with impunity. Where we came from you sat quietly through films. You could laugh at the jokes, sure, but that was it. What you didn't do was show these sorts of emotions. Even if you felt them.

For some reason, the crowd's outburst caused me to abandon my escape plans. Suddenly, I wanted to be around for the next explosion, wanted to witness that frenzy once again. I wasn't disappointed. A few minutes later there was another scary scene and an even greater pandemonium erupted, a tempest of joyous fear that ended in relieved laughter. Kevin and I looked at each other and a secret understanding passed between us. This was great. We weren't going anywhere.

That first movie eventually ended in an orgy of on-screen carnage that was rivalled by the mayhem in the audience.

One kid even leapt on to the small stage to admonish the werewolf before being gently pulled away by a surprisingly patient usher. And then the film was over. The lights came up. I'd forgotten this was going to happen, that our cover of darkness would eventually be blown. But there we were, as white as grub worms beneath an upturned rock.

To my astonished relief, none of the other kids took any notice of us. Sure, a few did double takes, but that was it. They were too busy laughing and jostling each other, too giddy with the horror they'd just let themselves experience. I realised that Kevin and I were safe here, that as long as the kids around us were able to vent their terror at the screen then we would be all right. After all, who cares about a couple of scrawny white kids with bad haircuts when you have Vincent Price or Lon Chaney Jr to worry about. All of a sudden, *we* were the invisible ones.

The second film soon started and, as it unfolded, something else strange began to happen. It was a cheap vampire flick, something Kevin and I would have scoffed at had we seen it anywhere else. But now, sitting in this cavernous old theatre, surrounded by hundreds of raucous kids, we found ourselves becoming genuinely frightened by what we saw. To coin a phrase, the fear in the Roxy was infectious. Several times we jumped from our seats, and Kevin clutched my arm at one point, only to pull his hand quickly away in confused embarrassment. We even managed a few tentative shouts near the film's end, although they were lost in the general din.

And so it went for the rest of that first Saturday. By the end of *Them!* we were hooked, scared to death and having the time of our young lives. When I came out I felt better than I had in a long time. We merely shrugged when Kevin's father asked if we'd had fun. This was something we didn't want our parents to know about.

* * *

The next Saturday we went again, secretly this time. The same old man was there behind the counter, smiling at us with his eyes as we bought our Goobers and Nehi. And the films proved just as frightening as last time. We shouted and yelled and squirmed along with everyone else, the caution and reserve we'd been taught all our lives making way for this more natural response. After all, what we did, what all the kids at the Roxy were doing, made perfect sense. It was a scary movie. You let yourself be scared. And then, when you tumbled giddily on to the street after the lights came up, everything else in your life, girls and parents and all that bad news on TV, didn't seem quite so terrifying.

It was after we'd gone four or five times that everything changed. It was a warm April evening when it happened, a Wednesday I think. Mom was doing the dishes and Dad was reading the paper and I was watching TV. Suddenly, the show was interrupted by a special report. Someone named King was dead. I was confused – this was America, we didn't have kings here. But then they showed a photo of a man I'd seen before, a black preacher with a kind face and a musical voice. Other images began to appear – men crouching on a hotel balcony, a row of burning buildings, armed police scouring rooftops for a sniper.

'I'm scared, John,' my mom said, wringing her sudsy hands.

'I don't think they'll come up here,' my dad answered, though his voice was anything but certain.

Later that night, when I was supposed to be asleep, I heard voices outside my window. I got out of bed and looked, fearing 'they' had indeed arrived, whoever 'they' were. But it was just my dad and some other fathers, gathered at the bottom of the street. Two cars were parked face to face, blocking off the entrance. A few of the men held hunting rifles, their stern faces underlit by the cars' headlights. It reminded me of a scene from that first film we'd seen at the Roxy, where a group of townsfolk had gone hunting for the werewolf. In the distance I could hear the wail of a siren, matched by another, like a mating call. Wavering light began to shine above downtown and for a moment I wondered if the Roxy was on fire. My mother joined me at the window.

'The governor's called out the National Guard,' she explained, stroking my unruly hair. 'We'll be all right.'

The next day everything was quiet. Our car was back in the driveway, our dads were at work, those hunting rifles were locked away. On the news that evening there was more stuff about burning buildings and black guys getting arrested but that all seemed very far away. There were a few more sirens late that night but they soon died down. And the sky above downtown was black as a theatre in that moment just before the film starts, the moment after the lights go down.

The next Saturday I went by Kevin's house to pick him up for our usual session at the Roxy. He looked at me like I was crazy. Go downtown? After what had happened? No way, he said, before going back inside to watch TV. I knew I should do the same but for some reason I had to see if the Roxy had been consumed by those fires.

Downtown was quieter than normal. Broken glass covered the sidewalks and a few buildings had been reduced to ashes. As riots go ours had been a modest affair, nothing like the conflagrations that hit Detroit or Newark. And, most importantly, the Roxy was still intact. Though I knew I should probably go home, for some reason I bought my ticket and crossed the big lobby, starting to feel that everything was going to be like it was before. But the moment I got to the concession counter I knew I was wrong. The old man's eyes weren't smiling this time, they were cold and distant. When I asked him for my usual box of Goobers he simply shook his head.

'Ain't got no candy today,' he said. 'No drinks neither.'

I looked at the shelves between us – there was enough confectionery there to feed a stadium full of kids. But something in the old man's eyes kept me from arguing. I simply nodded and went into the theatre, taking my usual front row seat. The movie was *The Creature from the Black Lagoon*. A classic, scarier than anything we'd yet seen. It wasn't long until the growing tension and swelling music overtook me, so that when the creature finally made his first appearance out of the primal ooze, I instinctively let out a whoop, the sort that would normally have been subsumed in the general chaos. But today it rang out through the great, silent hall like a single gun shot. I turned, wondering for a moment if perhaps the theatre was empty. Hundreds of pairs of angry eyes met my stare. I turned and sank into my seat.

And so it went for the rest of the film. Even during the most climactic scenes, the only response was utter stillness, utter silence. I badly wanted to stand up on my seat and shout, to kick-start the fear. But I didn't, of course. Even then, at the age of nine, when there was so little about the world I understood, I knew that something had changed, that the Saturday morning ritual of horror was over. These kids wouldn't be able to afford themselves the luxury of joyous terror for a long, long time. The good fear was gone from the Roxy now, replaced by the real thing.

On screen, the final battle began. But I didn't care. Suddenly, I felt too old for this. You had to be crazy to find this scary, what with all that was happening out there in the real world. And so, before the end of the movie, knowing all eyes were on me, knowing who the real monster at the Roxy was, I snuck out through the emergency exit and walked quickly back to my side of town.

Gewürztraminer

James Hamilton-Paterson

James Hamilton-Paterson was educated at Oxford, where he won the Newdigate Prize. He has written extensively for *The Sunday Times, Times Literary Supplement* and the *New Statesman*. He has published three works of non-fiction, two volumes of poetry and five novels, and is now writing a book about the senses. He is a Fellow of the Royal Geographical Society and lives in Italy and the Far East.

GEWÜRZTRAMINER was first broadcast on Radio 3.

∫

Gewürztraminer

It was inevitable that the Elgins and the Langlands would wind up as near-neighbours in London. The wives were fated to have been at school together just as their children were destined to dislike one another intensely at Holland Park Comprehensive. Neither family could remember exactly when they'd first met. They had probably drifted into each other's ambit via the early-morning swims which Jimmy and Nick sometimes took in the local baths. Fate had stopped short of decreeing the two men should be colleagues but they did work for rival newspapers, albeit in different capacities. Nick Langland ran an Arts page while Jimmy Elgin was more or less a turf correspondent.

Rivalry is really a form of love; and like the best marriages, good rivalries are made in heaven. Nick thought Jimmy was dangerously close to being a bit flash while probably making a fortune on the horses. Jimmy thought Nick despised him from the social heights of his arty celebrities while drifting around the Continent on a succession of grand freebies. Neither was completely wrong, though each was getting less money than the other feared. Mind you, Nick would have found this hard to believe of Jimmy Elgin, largely because of an episode which still rankled. A couple of years ago Nick had woken Amanda by shouting 'Gewürztraminer!' in his sleep. They'd laughed about it at breakfast, Amanda saying she'd married a man whose unconscious worked for Oddbins or Peter Dominic, but then Nick noticed a horse of that name was due to run in the Derby later that week. When he saw Jimmy at the baths next day he asked him to put a fifty pounds flutter on it for him. The expert warned him that only because it had a leg at each corner could one recognise it as a horse, but Nick insisted. Jimmy agreed but refused to take any money, however, explaining that it would be so much more satisfying to be paid when Nick had lost it. And then, confounding the pundits, Gewürztraminer won. Nick couldn't believe his luck until he caught up with Jimmy and the journalist smote a hand to his brow.

'Oh my God,' he said. 'I completely forgot, Nick. Can you believe I totally and utterly forgot to put your bet on? That nag was such a hopeless outsider. How are you ever going to forgive me?'

It would have been better had Amanda not bumped into Jimmy's wife Stephanie some weeks later and heard that the Elgins were negotiating for a little property in Tuscany thanks to a premium bond, a dead aunt and a lucky flier on the Derby.

'Complete fluke, that,' Stephanie admitted. 'Jimmy had this tip-off from a stable-boy about a rank outsider called Gewürztraminer and played a hunch. Well, they're professionals, aren't they? These hunches sometimes pay off. It's beyond people like you and me.'

Amanda could practically feel the relays clicking in her brain but she kept quiet. Since then the Langlands had heard a good deal about the Elgins' Tuscan cottage – a chaotic ruin, of course, but utterly sublime.

'Bet you it isn't,' Amanda said.

Maybe after all Jimmy did have a conscience about Nick's failed Derby for one day at the baths he asked:

'You lot going away in July? I suppose you wouldn't fancy a fortnight in our cottage? Buckshee, of course. You'd have the place to yourselves.'

'Why, that's very kind, Jimmy. I'm not sure . . .' Nick began. 'I mean, if you're really serious . . . Fact is, Amanda and I have rather cocked it up this year. *She* thought I was booking the holiday and *I* thought etcetera etcetera. But aren't you going to be needing the house yourselves?'

'Not in the last fortnight in July. Stephanie rashly promised Clarissa we'd take her to, God, wait for it, *Disneyland*, and she won't let us wriggle out. We'll be in Florida.'

Many conversations and several weeks later brought the Langland family to the terrace of an old stone house on the edge of a sunny gulf. Thickly wooded hillside fell away at their feet and subsided in yellow fields of sunflowers several miles away, which was also the distance to the nearest neighbour.

'Golly,' said Amanda. 'We will try not to be envious, won't we?'

'Gewürztraminer,' said Nick pungently, using a word he had adopted as his private expletive. 'This is why they wanted us here.'

'This it?' asked Daniel, having just consented to get out of the car where he'd been playing an electronic game. 'You mean we've got to spend two whole weeks stuck up here? I want to go swimming.'

'You've only just arrived,' Amanda protested. 'There's the car to unpack first. We haven't even explored the house. We'll go tomorrow, Danny. Promise.'

'What's this hole, then, Mummy?'

Before they'd left London Stephanie had given them a wad of handwritten Useful Hints which explained, among much else, that the large pit they'd find excavated a few yards from the front steps was in readiness for a half-grown walnut tree to replace the one on the far side of the house dying of old age. Clearly the Elgins were not about to wait for nature to do her stuff in the usual slow motion. An instant tree, they wanted, not some sapling; so a tree they would have.

What they had claimed about the house itself was absolutely true: it was a basic old stone farmhouse with four rooms upstairs and four stables down. There was nothing fancy about it though Nick and Amanda reluctantly had to agree they were restoring it with surprising taste. What was quite exceptional was simply its position. The stupendous isolation and panorama made the house feel as ancient as it must have been, stuck up on a mountainside above the twentieth century whose contaminations had not yet risen high enough to damage a silence which still belonged to another era.

'Blast them,' said Nick as they lay in the Elgins' bed that night listening to nothing but the sound of owls coming with a warm breeze through the open window. 'What idiots we were. We ought to have known better.'

'Yes, well,' sighed Amanda. 'It's a free fortnight, Nicky. Look at it that way.'

By the time the Langlands were halfway through the fortnight even Daniel had succumbed to the charm of the place. That is to say he was more easily bought off by a daily trip down to the Olympic-sized swimming pool in the local town than his parents would have dared predict. A couple of hours there with the odd pizza or ice cream thrown in would pacify him. For the remainder of the day he was content to explore the roughly wooded hillside around the house, an intrepid ten-year-old armed with a cherished Swiss Army knife catching crickets and trying to hit butterflies on the wing with a catapult. One morning when he and Amanda had disappeared down the appalling unmade track and the Range Rover's brake lights vanished into the forest Nick sat on the terrace and pretended to work. It was hopeless. The view was too distracting. After half an hour his hand strayed down for the binoculars. He trained them on the two distant hill towns, one on either side, whose stonework glowed in the morning sunlight like patches of pale honey. 'What you're looking out over,' said Stephanie's user-friendly notes, 'is a pre-Roman landscape. Those little towns are Etruscan and not Roman at all. Imagine: they've been continuously lived in from anything up to eight centuries before Christ was even thought of. They're always finding— '

Nick threw down the stapled pages. Stephanie had probably copied it all out of some ghastly guide book but it was the proprietorial tone he couldn't bear. It wasn't enough that she'd bought ten acres of Tuscany; she wanted to appropriate the wretched Etruscans as well, plus about two and a half thousand years of history. For several minutes he toyed with the seductive fantasy of burning her house down. 'I say, Jimmy, I'm frightfully sorry. It looks as though there was a leak in your Calor gas system. That's what the firemen think, anyway.' He wondered how much he'd have to slip the firemen for them to stick to the story . . . Oh well, it was a nice idea. Not only did he lack the mean ruthlessness to do such a thing but a burnt stone house could be reconstructed. Its site would remain unchanged; and if position meant everything then this house was essentially indestructible. Gewürztraminer, frankly.

When the others returned they all had a leisurely lunch on the terrace. Nick and Amanda drank perhaps just a couple of glasses of wine too many which brought on a disinclination to do anything much for several hours, so they went upstairs for a siesta. For a moment Nick leaned sleepily on the window sill looking down at the vines covering the pergola immediately beneath. It was all too much. Through the gaps he could glimpse Daniel squatting at the bottom of the hole by the front steps trying to stab a lizard with his Swiss Army knife. What rotten vindictive little creatures children were, he thought as he tottered to the bed. Why couldn't they live in harmony, and so on and so forth . . .? He and Amanda slept and then both came wide awake at the same moment.

'Did you just wake?' Nick asked.

'Yes. There wasn't a noise, was there?'

'I didn't hear anything. Just something Danny's up to, probably.'

Worried enough to get up and check, she went down to the front steps. There lay Danny's catapult with a small heap of stones. Then from practically at her feet she heard a strange sound, half sob and half shout, hollow and muffled. 'Darling?' she called. 'Danny? Is that you?'

'I can't get out,' came his voice. 'Get me out, Mummy.'

Then she saw the irregular dark hole near the bottom of the excavated pit.

'Oh my God, Danny! Are you all right? Wait, don't move . . . *Nick*! Quickly!'

There followed five minutes of the traditional frantic advice, entreaties, orders, scurryings, countermandings and suchlike, in the course of which a torch was found. Amanda crawled gingerly down the side of the pit to the hole while Nick held her ankles. With the Tuscan sunlight blotted out by her own head and shoulders the torch's weak beam revealed Danny's upturned face about ten feet below her own, tiny in the bowels of the earth. His nose was bleeding but otherwise he seemed unharmed.

'Hang on, darling,' she said. 'We'll soon have you out. Can you see anything down there?'

'Not now,' he said. She scrabbled backwards enough to let the sunlight in again. 'It's sort of a cellar, I think.'

'Is it safe for you to move back a bit if we try to get a rope down?'

'Dunno,' he called. 'I don't like it down here, Mummy. I want to come up.'

'I know, darling, but this hole might collapse some more and you don't want to be standing right underneath, do you? Just a sec . . . Nick!' she called. 'Help me up and fetch a ladder.'

Another five minutes.

'How the hell can you renovate a house without a bloody ladder?' demanded Nick, panting. 'Typical Elgins. Incompetent cheapskates. And they won't have a rope either, I'll bet.' This turned out to be another bet he would have won. He did find a length of string, though, and lowered the torch to his trapped son. '"So lovely to be off the phone", didn't Stephanie say? It's wonderful. You stay here and keep Danny company and I'll go and get the fire brigade or something. That place near the swimming pool, isn't that the Carabinieri? Don't worry, I'll find someone.'

He did, returning after forty minutes with four firemen who were kindness and efficiency itself. They laid a short ladder across the pit and lowered a rope with a canvas sling on the end. Within a couple of minutes Danny emerged, blinking in the sunlight, covered in smears of earth and blood.

'An ambulance is on its way,' said Nick, but Amanda soon ascertained that it wouldn't be needed. A bath would do just fine, she said, and took the boy off. He seemed far more put out at having lost his Swiss Army knife than bothered by his ordeal. His voice could be heard from an upstairs window accompanied by the sound of running water, explaining that when the hole suddenly opened up beneath him he must have let go of the knife.

His father was still fervently thanking the rescuers in Home Counties Italian when the ambulance arrived. Its crew were visibly disappointed at having come all the way for nothing worse than a nosebleed. Children who fell down wells were, thank God, rare; but when they did there was guaranteed newspaper coverage with pictures. This was evidently not to be one of those occasions. On the other hand there might be some mileage in the story after all. What was this hole, anyway, if it wasn't a well? After cigarettes and discussion one of the firemen put on a safety harness and was lowered back into the shallow pit. He enlarged the hole, was handed down an immense yellow lamp and vanished into Daniel's recent dungeon. In due course when the boy emerged from the house looking considerably cleaner than when he'd gone in he was treated to an effusive welcome.

'They're saying you're a hero, Danny,' explained his father. 'It seems you've made an archaeological discovery. They think you've found an Etruscan tomb.'

'A *tomb*? *Errch*! You mean I was down there with dead corpses?'

'No, it's just an empty burial chamber. Apparently there's one in town, too, but yours is far and away better. Well done, Danny.'

'How absolutely sickening,' was Amanda's reaction. 'A house, a view, and now a historical bloody monument thrown in as well.'

'Will there be a reward?' Danny asked.

'Bound to be,' said Nick.

'That's good. Then I can get a bigger Swiss Army knife.'

'If what I'm thinking turns out to be right,' his father said, 'I'll cheerfully buy you the entire Swiss Army.'

It was not long before his optimism began to be justified. First thing next morning the local press arrived, followed by the Mayor and several men introduced as 'historical experts'. More people descended the hole, more startled cries drifted up. Nick himself volunteered to go down and found a small vaulted chamber looking pretty much as he'd imagined it would, with a ragged hole in one corner of the ceiling. It seemed unremarkable except for black beetles.

'This is awful,' said Amanda as they were clearing up after a late lunch and the sound of revving engines became once again audible on the track below. 'Someone else is coming. I do wish they'd leave us in peace.'

'I do hope they won't,' Nick said fervently, and explained to her the true thickness of the silver lining.

Five hectic days later, springy with suppressed glee, he was down at the local station to welcome the Elgins back from Disneyland. When their train at last drew in he could barely stop himself bounding over to where Jimmy, Stephanie and Clarissa were getting out.

'So,' he greeted them, 'how was Disneyland?'

'Great,' said Stephanie. 'Wasn't it, Rissa?'

'Frankly,' Jimmy said, 'it's nice to be back in Tuscany.'

'Well, your famous house awaits you.'

'It's not bad, really, is it? Did you all have a good time, Nick?'

'I'm not exaggerating when I say we've had the time of our lives. Living in such style you wouldn't believe. Photographers, interviewers, Men from the Ministry . . .'

'What on earth are you talking about?'

So then and there in the station forecourt Nick broke the news that the Elgins were the proud possessors of an Etruscan hypogea which some expert from the Antiquities Department in Siena had declared was perfectly preserved and of the greatest archaeological importance. 'Honestly, you lot,' he finished, 'you are jammy. You not only chance on the most fabulous house but you get an ancient tomb into the bargain. Listen, you'll be itching to get up there.

Here are the keys. We've left it all in running order as per., but do be careful of the hole. I'm afraid we've got to dash off to Florence now. We'll see each other back in London, OK? And we really can't thank you enough. Bye . . . Bye, Rissa.'

'I mean of course they *are* jammy,' Nick said later as they sat down to dinner in Florence. 'But it's good jam that gives nobody any ill wind. My Italian's far from perfect but as I understand it they're pretty much lumbered. I believe archaeological sites automatically belong to the State. If they're on private property the landowner has to guarantee access to the public. Bang goes that fabulous privacy, for a start. It'll be like living in Pompeii. Then I think it has to be open pretty much all the year round, so if they want to keep the house they'll either have to move there permanently or pay for a live-in caretaker. And if they do decide to sell I doubt they'll get much more than they paid for it despite all that work. It's got Etruscan blight. I think we won that one . . . Sorry, Danny? I told you: you can have absolutely anything on the menu you want. Only don't make yourself too sick because tomorrow we're going to ransack Florence for as many Swiss Army knives with as many blades as you feel you'll need for the rest of your life. And Amanda, darling, a suggestion. Were we going to have white wine?'

'I thought a chilled Frascati would go down well.'

'It would,' agreed Nick. 'But my money's on a really decent bottle of Gewürztraminer.'

Bertram's Funeral

Allan Massie

Allan Massie was born in Singapore in 1938, brought up in Aberdeenshire and educated at Glenalmond and Trinity College, Cambridge.

He is the *Scotsman*'s lead fiction-reviewer, a columnist and reviewer for the *Daily Telegraph*, a Fellow of the Royal Society of Literature and has been a Booker Prize judge. His novels include THE LAST PEACOCK, which won the Frederick Niven Award in 1981, A QUESTION OF LOYALTIES, winner of the Saltire Society/*Scotsman* Book of the Year Award, CAESAR and most recently THE RAGGED LION.

He is married, has three children, and lives in the Scottish Borders.

BERTRAM'S FUNERAL was read by David Burke, and broadcast on Radio 4.

ſ

Bertram's Funeral

They knew him in the village as 'the writer', but none of them had read his books. That didn't make them remarkable. His success, once considerable, was a bit back. When he brought out a novel now, it was reviewed as one in a batch, often at the tail-end, and his telephone didn't ring. He read interviews with more fashionable novelists instead.

The cottage garden was overgrown and the wind bent the brown thistle-heads. It was too early for a gin. Most days that wouldn't have bothered or stopped him, but he was going to the funeral of an old friend. He didn't want to topple into the grave.

The old friend was a painter. When Graham started out as a writer, he had known people who went and did all sorts of different things. His own father had been an engineer and the people he put in his first two books were engaged in the sort of occupations that demand regular hours; he had characters who wouldn't themselves read novels. Now he knew only other writers, painters, failed actresses, and the layabouts drawing dole money who were numerous in the county where he had come to live. That was after his wife left him, or he left her – he couldn't be sure which had made the decisive move, if indeed there had been one – the marriage came to the point when there were no leaves left on the tree.

The cat came to the window. He let it in and it asked for food. He scratched it behind the ear, but it shook its head, and he went to the refrigerator and took a chunk of cod he had cooked yesterday and put some on a saucer. He gave himself that gin to keep the cat company.

It was a beautiful cat, a long-haired Red Self, half Persian. He had swithered about having him neutered, and then done nothing, and put up with the spraying. The cat was called Trajan, after the emperor, and slept on Graham's bed and sometimes nibbled his ear in the dark.

The church was five miles away. He drove through the lanes at twenty-five miles an hour, hooting at junctions. He sat upright in his big black car. The wings were spattered with mud. He had had the car twenty years, and the marque was long discontinued as a result of a series of mergers and what they called rationalisations. It would last some time yet. He didn't do 3,000 miles in a year and usually he remembered to garage it in the old barn which went with the cottage. He sang, off-key, as he drove:

> We plough the fields and scatter
> The good seed on the land,
> But it is fed and watered
> By God's almighty hand . . .

He didn't go to church now, except for funerals, but he sang hymns while driving, shaving, or taking a bath.

There were already a lot of people in the church, and, in the English fashion, they had filled it from the back, so that he had to advance well up the aisle to find a place. He dropped on his knees on a worn hassock, extruding stuffing, to say a long-remembered, long-disused prayer. 'Visit this habitation, we beseech thee, o Lord . . .' Why did the word, 'beseech', vanished from ordinary parlance, where, in any case, if used, it would be condemned as feeble, sound so right here?

He sat back and fingered his black tie. The last funeral he had attended, he had been the only man wearing a black tie, and he had hesitated before knotting it this morning. He had looked at himself in the glass, with the tie dangling loose, at the face he had not liked when young, though some found it attractive, but which he had grown fond of as it deteriorated, and then he had sighed, and knotted the tie, thinking, as he seldom did, of his mother who used to ask if he had put on clean underclothes in case he was knocked down by a car and taken to hospital.

There was a good turn-out for Bertram. Graham had been to services at crematoria where there had been so few that a hymn was out of the question. He made a point of going to the funerals of friends, and there were a lot of them now as gin, whisky, cigarettes, anxiety, loss of hope, took their toll. He hated crematoria though. The assumption there was that the dead were simply inconveniences to be shuffled off; his presence was a silent protest.

A woman, heavily veiled, was advancing up the aisle. That was perhaps a bit much. One of Bertram's old mistresses making a point, staking a claim, stealing the scene? Then she passed him and he saw it was a young black man with dreadlocks. The trailing skirt he had caught in the corner of his eye belonged to an overcoat. The young man's head was bowed which was why it had looked as if he was wearing a veil. Graham felt a giggle steal up on him: it was a joke Bertram would have liked.

Besides the mistresses, Bertram had had three wives, not concurrently, and six or seven children. There might have been other children born out of wedlock, Graham didn't know. He had scattered his image freely enough. Graham made a sign to Annie, the second wife, the one he had known best and liked least.

The vicar read the Twenty-third Psalm, from green pastures to the valley of the shadow of death. Tears came into Graham's eyes. Another lesson: in my Father's house are many mansions . . . as many, he wondered, as the bed-sitters of Pimlico, where he had been living in a drab room with yellow walls, when he had first met Bertram? He had shared it with a young man called Richard. Neither of them had any work, but they spoke of how they would dominate the world. One evening, Richard said: 'Do you and Bertram have to be drunk every night?'

They stood to sing. 'The ancient Prince of hell/Hath risen with purpose fell . . .' 'Ein festes burg ist unser Gott . . .' In his youth Graham worked at night, often finishing at two, three in the morning. Then he went out into the city and walked. It was a time when even the bad things that happened seemed fruitful.

'The blessing of God Almighty, Father, Son and Holy Ghost . . .' Eight young men, at least three of them Bertram's sons, carried the coffin out of the church.

The rain had stopped. Bertram had loved painting rain. He did it well, better than anything else. There was one painting he had kept for years, refusing to sell, of ploughed fields in rain. The fields rose from the bottom of the canvas towards a line of winter trees. It was grey and brown, half a dozen different greys and browns, except for a dot of pink placed by a church spire that rose between the trees. There was a figure in the foreground, but Graham couldn't remember if it had been male or female. It didn't matter. It was just there, and maybe it was meant to be insignificant. Then Bertram sold the painting and probably it was hung in an American gallery now.

He squashed his hat onto his head and buttoned his overcoat. It was an eastern county and all winds were sharp from October to March. There was a big sky and the chug of a tractor. Jackdaws flew about the little church with its square tower. He was standing near a woman whom he recognised as his daughter. He hadn't seen her for six or seven years, and the line of her jaw was stronger than it used to be. She hadn't seen him, her gaze was fixed on the grave. Old words floated towards him. He took off his hat and shoved it into his pocket. He bent his head. Bertram was her godfather. That was why she was here, and it was right. They would have to speak, later. He used to call her 'Nutkin'. He doubted if she would like to be called 'Nutkin' now. Her coat was good and expensive. She had her arm round a young blond boy. It must be his grandson.

One of the young men holding one of the cords let go too soon. The coffin lurched feet first into the hole. For a moment it looked as if Bertram would have to be buried vertical. Then adjustments were made. The descent was accomplished. Handfuls of earth were thrown. The crowd began to disperse. Graham waited, then scratched up some of the blue-grey clay soil, and let it fall on his friend. That was that. He wondered if they had put a paint brush and palette in the coffin. He hoped they had, not that he would ask for a typewriter in his. There wouldn't be this sort of turn-out when it came to his turn to turn in.

He touched his daughter on the shoulder.

'Susie,' he said, not daring 'Nutkin'.

His fingers left smears of clay on the good navy-blue cloth. He hoped she wouldn't notice till she got home and that she wouldn't then connect it with him.

'You should have let me know you were coming. I'd have given you lunch.'

The boy was looking at him. He had the kind of face illustrators used to draw in school stories, for the hero – frank, open, manly; obsolete, unusable epithets. Graham thought of other boys he knew, or saw around on his rare visits to London, and wondered how long this boy could keep that look in today's world.

Susie said nothing. She left the word 'lunch' hanging in the thin autumn air.

'You don't know me,' he said to the boy. 'I'm your grand-father.'

How old was he? Thirteen, fourteen? Something like that. He was a nice-looking boy, and he had nice manners, because he smiled now, not embarrassed, even as if pleased to meet him.

'This is the first funeral I've ever been to,' he said. 'I've only come because I'm on half-term.'

'Good,' Graham said. 'I'm glad you've come, Susie. Old Bertram was always fond of you.'

'He sent me a painting last Christmas,' she said. 'I could see it was good, but I only hang abstracts. But he said it was valuable and I suppose it is.'

'Take it to his dealer if you want it valued. But I should hang on to it. Bertram said his paintings will be worth more in ten, fifteen years than they are now. That was quite recently. He always had a good eye for market values.'

He hoped he didn't sound bitter. The words could seem bitter, but they weren't meant that way. Still, they helped get over the awkwardness and ease them on their way from the churchyard to the house. But the awkwardness couldn't be altogether avoided.

'Is your mother here? I didn't see her in the church.'

It was mad that he hadn't thought they might be here.

'No,' she said. 'She's not. In fact, she's ill. In fact she's in hospital.'

The wind twitched at the thin branches, ruffled his hair. He pushed his hat back on his head.

'I'm sorry,' he said. 'Is it serious?'

'Only tests. They're doing tests.'

'Nutkin', he thought again. I suppose she really does dislike me. He ought to know which school the boy was at.

'Tests?' he said.

'Yes,' she said. 'It begins with tests, doesn't it?'

Falling

Susan Johnson

Susan Johnson was born in Brisbane in 1956, and grew up in Sydney. She worked as a journalist before turning to fiction full-time. Her short stories have appeared in a number of Australian literary journals and magazines and her novels include MESSAGES FROM CHAOS, FLYING LESSONS and, most recently, A BIG LIFE. She lives with her husband in London.

FALLING was read by Tara Dominick and broadcast on Radio 4.

$\int$

Falling

On summer nights, as soon as Mrs Jenny Saunders closed her eyes, she heard the long mechanical breath of Hong Kong. She heard fat metal boxes sucking clean breath from the air, one long inhalation without lull. She lay on her back listening to the roar, imagining the sky sucked out, leaving a hole where heaven used to be.

All summer long Mrs Jenny Saunders lay surrounded by artificial air, the great city's mechanical breath pulsing in her ears, dreaming of a hole above.

Mrs Jenny Saunders had not always dreamt of absence. She had once had long blonde hair and a knowledge of her own lustre. At twenty-three Mrs Jenny Saunders had strode London streets convinced of success, brandishing her pretty face like a blade.

Martin Saunders had not fallen at once: instead, he tossed his dark blond hair back from his forehead and considered himself too young to marry. Yet he had looked at Mrs Jenny Saunders and seen her winner's eye: he invited her in but did not yet close the door. He continued to go out with other girls and ate the required number of dinners at Temple, before qualifying as a barrister at twenty-seven.

Not long after his twenty-eighth birthday, Martin Saunders and Mrs Jenny Saunders were finally married, mainly due to the skilful arts of Mrs Jenny Saunders. She viewed Martin Saunders as a kind of active weapon and herself as a reconnaissance soldier: she did not so much negotiate with him as steer him by covert means in the direction she wished him to go.

Soon after the wedding Martin Saunders was offered a position with the Hong Kong government on a very high salary: Mrs Jenny Saunders saw immediately he meant to take it. She had never been to Hong Kong and had in mind an old colonial-style house with endless gardens, and Chinese servants moving silently in slippers.

Whenever Mrs Jenny Saunders thought of those first years in Hong Kong she saw herself walking on an endless concrete walkway, moving from air-conditioned building to air-conditioned building. She seemed to have spent a long time waiting in the lobbies of international hotels and in restaurants on the top of tall buildings.

There was often mist in the hills behind the city, a blue haze cast over everything. Mrs Jenny Saunders quickly found a flat for them in a highrise called 'Elegant Gardens' and a young Filipina maid, Miss Ophelia Flora Fernando, came to live in the small room behind the kitchen. Ophelia had trouble distinguishing between 'he' and 'she', because her own language used one word for both. Mrs Jenny Saunders considered Ophelia a rather silly girl and did her best to ignore her endless chatter. Nonetheless she could not help watching as Ophelia hung out the washing on brightly coloured poles from their twenty-fourth floor window, talking to other Filipina maids leaning from windows while she did so. This was how Ophelia heard the story one morning of the old Chinese woman who had fallen from Mr and Mrs Saunders' flat and had been miraculously caught on some sheets hanging out to dry nine floors below.

'He was like a baby delivered by the stork,' Ophelia repeated to Mrs Jenny Saunders, 'an old Chinese baby, shouting he was Ma'am, shouting!' Ophelia giggled and leant perilously from the waist out the window to place a towel on a yellow pole.

Mrs Jenny Saunders felt her first slow vertiginous pull towards the concrete, and it was after this that she began to trace a path as far away as possible from windows.

Mrs Jenny Saunders learnt to cook and made girlfriends when she attended French cooking classes. Her girlfriends all had husbands who worked for petrol companies and had sumptuous company flats on The Peak. Some of them had lived in Singapore or obscure Arab states; they had ridden the golden ponies of Arab kings.

Mrs Jenny Saunders listened, moving amongst them, and felt her own life to be lucky. She sometimes had unworthy thoughts about the girls of West Dulwich she had left behind, who must be struggling now on mortgages with unsuccessful husbands.

It soon became clear to Mrs Jenny Saunders that it was time to have a baby, to move into the next stage of her life plan. But to her great surprise no baby came: a year passed, then another, and another, Martin Sauders began to make noises about Mrs Jenny Saunders wasting time and for the first time she felt the flush of panic. 'Just what do you do all day?' Martin Saunders enquired crossly, but when Mrs Jenny Saunders tried to explain he rolled his eyes and blew air from his mouth in exasperation.

When Mrs Jenny Saunders laid out the details of her day to her husband it did not seem like a lot of work even to her, yet she could not explain how she seemed to be constantly rushing; shopping, planning dinner parties, cooking. Before her marriage Mrs Jenny Saunders had only done this and that, for she had never once imagined she would need a full-time career.

It was about this time that Mrs Jenny Saunders saw her husband from a distance in the street. She was about to make some sign but saw that he was with a young barrister from his office, a pretty Chinese girl from Taiwan. Even from a distance Mrs Jenny Saunders saw Martin Saunders' proprietorial hand guide Ms Florence Wong to a taxi and give her Armani-suited bottom a playful thwack.

Mrs Jenny Saunders suddenly found she did not enjoy having the maid Ophelia under her feet all day, so she took up walking. At first she walked in endless shopping complexes which all seemed to be joined like a maze, and imagined navigating the entire circumference of Hong Kong without once emerging into open air.

But she soon grew tired of false air and emerged into the streets, breathing. Away from the main Western business centre Hong Kong had been recaptured by the Chinese: pigs' hearts swung on metal hooks, the lungs of unknown creatures were hosed out on pavements so that the pressure of water made them once again rise and fall. Mrs Jenny Saunders jumped out of the way when a young man threw into the gutter a twirl of snake intestine: it went on moving, a muscle without brain.

She followed men with ducks on poles, strung up by their strangled necks; she followed bent women selling oranges. Everywhere she smelt incense and saw offerings to gods; in her ears she heard human voices. Before long the angular tones of Cantonese became as familiar to her as the roar of cars or the straining engines of buses.

When Mrs Jenny Saunders realised she was pregnant she could not help but think that here at last was her salvation. Martin Saunders surprised her by being swell-chested and telling everyone who was important. He appeared to like the image of himself as a man with an attractive wife and a child and immediately began to talk of the merits of boarding schools in England.

It was decided that Mrs Jenny Saunders would fly home to London for the birth and that her husband would join her as soon as the baby was born.

While Mrs Jenny Saunders was flying over countries, she looked down through the clouds imagining how it would feel to fall. It might be a swooping, gentle motion, or a jerk of the stomach as when going over an unexpected hill.

Mrs Jenny Saunders held her living belly, telling the watery creature inside that it was not yet time to dive.

After the baby was born Martin Saunders came as soon as he could, holding Mrs Jenny Saunders' hand while she refused to cry. He told her that he would make suitable arrangements for the infant and that it would all turn out for the best, and no one need mention it once they were back home. Mrs Jenny Saunders heard him but was thinking of her son's strange flat eyes, his features which looked oddly Chinese. He had looked straight up at her and she had said, 'Can you take him away,' for she had not counted on the accuracy of his vision. Mrs Jenny Saunders did not wish to look upon this failure of her body and felt only relief when his weight was gone. Yet she imagined she could pick out his cry when she walked down the corridor. It was harsher, more bitter.

At night she dreamt of a falling baby caught by a sheet; it had an old face and did not make a sound.

After a decent interval Mrs Jenny Saunders returned to Hong Kong. When one of her girlfriends tried to say how sorry she was, Mrs Jenny Saunders put out her hand and gently said, 'Please.' After this no one spoke of it, although for a while Mrs Jenny Saunders noticed covert glances in her direction whenever anyone mentioned babies.

One day Mrs Jenny Saunders looked in the mirror and saw with some surprise she was getting old. She stared at her reflection for a long time before turning away.

When Mrs Jenny Saunders fell pregnant again she waited until she had the results of the amniocentesis test before she told

Martin Saunders.

'It's all right,' she said when she saw fear on his face, 'this time everything's normal.'

Mrs Jenny Saunders did not go to England in a plane but gave birth to a perfect daughter in a hospital high on a Chinese hill. Martin Saunders kissed her cheek and said, 'Well done, darling. I'll take you to Gaddi's as soon as you're up and about.'

The baby was placid and rarely cried, yet Mrs Jenny Saunders was not drawn to her. She stood by the cot and looked down upon the blank, unwritten face and had no compulsion to know more. Instead, the maid Ophelia took the baby for hours at a time while Mrs Jenny Saunders resumed walking.

She walked up mountains, through crowded streets, she kept her head up to check the sky. It was during these long summer afternoons that it first occurred to Mrs Jenny Saunders that the sky had been sucked out, and she began to count every fat metal box she saw drawing the air from her very mouth. She saw how they chilled the air inside by robbing from the living, how they stole from nature to squander on the dead.

Before long the mechanical breath of the city began to intrude upon her dreams, so that she had to stay awake each night in a state of vigilance. It occurred to her that she was stranded in an unknown bed, a hostage in a spectral city with no moon and no stars. The baby in the next room did not make a sound, but Mrs Jenny Saunders knew it breathed too. She could faintly hear the high, bitter cry of another baby, far off, bound up somewhere far away.

On summer nights she prepared to slip from her skin and rise up into that cold absence, into the hole where heaven used to be. She imagined the cool rush of the air as she passed, the feel of movement against her skin. But Mrs Jenny Saunders always remembered just in time that no living woman was capable of falling upwards, and that the only way to fall properly was down.

The Matriarch of
Den Amstel

Roy Heath

Roy Heath is from Guyana and now lives in London. His novels include A MAN CAME HOME, THE MURDERER (winner of the *Guardian* Fiction Prize), and also OREALLA. His last novel was THE SHADOW BRIDE. In 1990 he published the first part of his autobiography SHADOWS ROUND THE MOON, and he is now working on the second instalment.

The Matriarch of Den Amstel was broadcast on Radio 4, and read by Hugh Quarshie.

The Matriarch of Den Amstel

Vibart and Stella were judged by their neighbours to be a family of eccentrics, because he had once experimented with the planting of wheat in his front garden and she hung the bed covers out of her back window in summer as she had been in the habit of doing before she left Guyana. I had met him in a Kilburn snooker club I frequented, a dingy hall which often bore evidence of violence from a previous night, broken cue rests, score panels wrenched from the wall, and once a spattering of blood on the green baize of our favourite table. He and I were chalk and cheese, he placid, apparently incapable of being roused, while I continually chafed at the misery of redundancy.

I knew Vibart liked the hall as much as I did, even though he never mentioned it in our conversations, laconic exchanges about our homeland and his two boy children.

'They had to learn how to work as soon as they could walk,' he once said, speaking of his offspring. And the three-year-old son came into the sitting-room, emptied the ash tray his father and I were sharing and then left without a word.

I returned to Vibart's house several times, but had met only his wife, a morose, taciturn young woman, and the younger son, who had emptied the ash tray. Then one Saturday evening on the occasion of a christening, he introduced me to his mother-in-law, a matriarch with slightly prominent teeth and a grand manner, who wore a white achal and fanned herself languidly. I could hardly keep my eyes off the old woman. The one point of repose in the room, she was surrounded by grown-ups and children dancing for all they were worth on that warm summer night.

She must have ordered someone to fetch the infant in whose honour the party was being held, for the next time I looked in her direction she was rocking it in her arms, her lace fan abandoned beside her on the couch. How could I explain the effect the old woman had on me? Sparing with gestures, almost expressionless, she nevertheless radiated a kind of magical authority that even managed to keep the infant asleep amidst the cigarette smoke, the throbbing music and a garish light from wall-lamps above her head.

Vibart's sister-in-law, Miranda, came up and introduced herself to me, on Vibart's orders as it turned out.

'Vibart say why you not dancing like everybody else. You just standing around drinking beer . . . I call Miranda. What's your name?'

I told her my name, slightly taken aback by her openness, which was in such contrast to the sister's distant manner. And immediately it occurred to me that I might even glean some information from her about the matriarch.

'Your mother,' I said, in an effort to make conversation, 'is. . .'

But, failing to find the right words to describe the old woman, I stopped in mid-sentence.

'She don't dance,' Miranda put in, misunderstanding my interest in her mother.

'Oh well,' I said, relieved.

I often danced with Miranda after that brief conversation; and during the interval when food was served on fragile plastic plates, we sat down on the top tread of the stairs and kept each other company. Then, emboldened by the beer I had been drinking, out of the blue I asked how long her mother had been living in England.

'A lil' more than three years,' she replied.

'And you?'

'Five years, but my sister has been here seven years. Oh, my mother din' want to come. Is a long story.'

Without prompting, she told how the old lady happened to leave Den Amstel, the village of her birth in Guyana, and travel across the sea to join her daughters and son-in-law in a London suburb. According to her there were many versions of the story, but she and her sister knew the facts, which they gleaned from acquaintances still living in Guyana and from her mother's mouth. Besides, their own part in the events could not be gainsaid.

'Well it happen like this,' Miranda began.

Mrs Saffon, her mother, had seen each of them off at Timehri airport without shedding a tear. Stella came abroad first and she, Miranda, followed two years later, to live with her sister, who had meanwhile married Vibart. As soon as she found work Miranda, encouraged by Stella's example, began sending their mother forty pounds every month; and even Vibart would dispatch a box of assorted goods from time to time, extending his affection for Stella to the lonely old lady.

None of them thought of calculating how much their mother actually needed, but rather regarded a tenth of their wages as an appropriate sum, following the practice of their Seventh Day Adventist friends, who gave as much to their church.

One evening, about a year after Miranda arrived in England, Vibart informed Stella that her mother had paid for the wedding of a poor village girl who was in the family way. The news came in a letter written to Vibart by his father, a notoriously unreliable newsmonger and a mischief-maker to boot.

'He so full of envy he can't bear to see anybody living good!' Vibart said.

But the seed of doubt had been sown. Perhaps her mother had not been banking the portion of the money she did not need, as they all expected.

'Tcha!' Miranda said, on being told the news. 'You know how Vibart father stay! He would bad-talk his own wife. Mama got more sense than all of us put together.'

And with that dismissal Stella's doubts were apparently laid to rest. Indeed, Miranda's assurances of their mother's good sense appeared to be borne out over a period of time by letters from various friends and relations, who made no mention of any extravagance on Mrs Saffon's part.

Life went on, the seasons merged one into the other like a player with many disguises, and Stella's first son was born on her mother's birthday, the 28th of February, when the almond trees were already in flower. The matriarch made him a wrist band of buck beads, which came with a friend who was travelling to see his father, long settled in London.

Stella's second son was born just fifteen months later, at a time when everyone had grown accustomed to a way of life that, at first sight apparently inappropriate to immigrants from a tropical country, now seemed as natural as the white flakes that sometimes settled on an icy ground in winter. There was no more talk of going back to Guyana for good, plans were made for the children's education, and Mrs Saffon, as far as they knew, had come to terms with living alone in her Den

Amstel cottage, littered with mementos of her emigrant children.

One Saturday morning Vibart came into the kitchen waving a letter the postman had just delivered. He put off reading it until Miranda called her sister from upstairs, then, with a solemn expression tore open the envelope, unfolded the letter, and announced that it was from Carstairs, an old Den Amstel village acquaintance.

'Carstairs say,' he began.

But, instead of continuing he fell silent, while reading the letter to himself.

As the women were to learn, their mother had defrayed the expenses of Carstairs' father's funeral and had also paid for a coach to transport all the old people of Den Amstel to the cemetery, since it had not ceased raining for four days.

The letter went on to relate how the poor villagers turned to her for succour in the hour of need. Since Stella and Miranda had gone away she had married off more than a score of acquaintances in Den Amstel and neighbouring villages, setting a Christian example that inspired everyone around her. Especially the old people, who could not get over the sudden popularity of marriage.

Miranda recalled how, when she and her sister were small children, their mother would take them to Creole functions as well as to East Indian rituals, and participated in both with the same fervour. She remembered vividly that on one occasion their mother danced in the centre of a Creole Ganda until, shaking to the sound of tambourines, she fell down in a trance and had to be put in the charge of two women.

But when the children became adolescents she grew more restrained, so much so that remarks were made about the change that had overtaken her, as though she were grieving for her young days.

Vibart opened the discussion that followed his disclosure of the letter's contents. Somebody would have to write to the old lady. If she were spending the money on herself, indulging her taste for stuffed crab-backs and imported wine, that would be one thing. But acting like a charitable organisation! Stella agreed with her husband, while Miranda, usually the most forthright in expressing her opinions, claimed with some hesitation that she was not certain they should risk offending the old lady. Mama was Mama! Perhaps she had the right to do as she pleased.

The discussion settled nothing and a week later no decision had yet been taken as to a suitable course of action. Meanwhile it never occurred to any of the three to reduce their monthly remittances to an amount which would provide well for the matriarch without creating a surplus that strangers could plunder.

In the end Vibart made a suggestion with which both his wife and sister-in-law fell in readily, less from conviction of its worth than in recognition of the need that something had to be done.

'Send for her! If she stay in Den Amstel, in a few years' time people goin' to be knocking 'pon her door demanding that she bury they dead.'

And Stella, the elder sister, undertook to write the letter which, they hoped, would wrench the matriarch from the village she had never left, and transplant her to an island of bleak perspectives.

The answer to Stella's letter did not come until three weeks later. Her mother would indeed like to be in England, for home was where her children lived.

Vibart's suggestion had borne fruit. Everyone was pleased, not least Stella's two sons, who were overjoyed at the news, imagining that, according to the story of their grandmother's extravagant generosity, the old lady was a source of undreamt-of benefits.

One October afternoon Vibart went to fetch her at the airport and she arrived in his car like some chauffeur-driven potentate. Stepping out on to the pavement, dressed in a printed cotton frock completely unsuited to the damp, autumnal air, she showed no sign of discomfort, nor made any complaint to her daughters, both of whom were wearing cardigans of knitted wool. And in her regal way she allowed herself to be kissed and fondled by them, while taking in the strange brick houses that pressed against one another.

Miranda stood up, having finished the story.

'Let's dance,' she suggested.

'Wait!' I said. 'What happened afterwards? Do you continue to give her money?'

'Of course!' she answered. 'She's our mother. But she does bank it in the Building Society.' Then, after hesitating for a while she said, 'Nowadays she does watch every penny.'

At this disclosure she turned to look at me, like someone who had just committed an indiscretion.

'I bet she misses Den Amstel,' I suggested, pretending that I had noticed nothing.

'Yes. But she want to be by us. She did go back a few months ago to Guyana on holiday. And d'you know? Her friends cleaned out her suitcases, even though she did bring them presents. They take everything, down to her hairbrush.'

I began to express sympathy, but Miranda corrected me.

'They're good people. They did fête her and entertain her the whole three weeks she was there.'

When the music began again we went back downstairs and joined the dancers among whom Stella's two boys were leaping about in the thick haze of smoke; and it occurred to me that the three-year-old would have his work cut out, collecting cigarette ends that littered the floor and stairs.

In the months that followed I visited the house frequently as my friendship with Vibart grew; but try as I might I was not able to get a word out of the matriarch; and I could not help thinking that there was an inner circle to which I did not belong, consisting exclusively of her family and people from Den Amstel.

Sometimes, in the murky silence of a winter's night, I imagine her looking down through the panes of a derelict suburban yard where once her son-in-law had grown wheat, to the consternation of his neighbours.

Damian's Day Out

Christopher Hope

Christoper Hope was born in Johannesburg. He has published five novels including A SEPARATE DEVELOPMENT, MY CHOCOLATE REDEEMER and SERENITY HOUSE. Works of non-fiction include WHITE BOY RUNNING and MOSCOW! MOSCOW!. The stories in his collections THE LOVE SONGS OF NATHAN J. SWIRSKY, were mostly commissioned by the BBC. A new novel, called IN DARKEST ENGLAND, will be published in the autumn.

DAMIAN'S DAY OUT was broadcast on Radio 4, and read by the author.

∫

Damian's Day Out

As Damian drove he sang. Under a violet sky which even the ozone filters in the anti-sun roof of his car could not sully, Damian filled his single lung with filtered air, sweetened with the scent of Norwegian pine, and sang his heart out.

To his left a field of geep, their goats' heads swivelling to watch him pass, their sheep's tails lifting as they turned. Identikit animals: gene-mixed, artificially mutated for lower fat and more flavour. Each with a neat yellow plastic Eurotag in its right ear. They reminded Damian of those fashions he dimly remembered from his youth when men and women wore a similar single yellow ring through their ear lobes.

Great and many, as they liked to say on the late night simulcasts devoted to the triumphs of science, great and many were the reasons why Damian should not have felt like singing. There was the endless, unstoppable rise of the rouble to which all major currencies were helplessly captive. The defection of the prime minister to China, though not unexpected, had been made worse by her statement that this is what her grandmother would have done but for misguided loyalty to her party, and her party had repaid her loyalty by dumping her. There was the tendency of the old king to weep in public whenever one of his trees died. The Moslem siege of Belgrade had entered its twentieth year.

But Damian sang even so. This was his day out. He was ninety years old with the flesh-to-bone ratio many would kill for. The face he saw in his rear-view video was round, full, relaxed, as the transponders buried in the road corrected his direction in a series of gentle shudders. Without demanding his carbon-dating ring, he could have passed for a man in early middle age. Follicly sound. True, he was an airbag short of full safety standards – but you could not see his missing lung and such was the sad prejudice of people still that it was only external imperfections that were jeered at in the streets. Only that morning the simulcast had told of a woman who coughed on the Maglev and was thrown from the car by furious passengers. Yet a politician who lied about his cerebral implant might well have kept his job, had he not been spotted by a team of headscanners on a surprise inspection.

The perfect fields slid by like well-made beds. To his left, glasshouses scarlet with non-bruising tomatoes. To his right, fields full of impervious cabbages, made safe by their scorpion poison genes from caterpillars. Yet there seemed no way of solving the inherent contradiction: the more health precautions you enforced, the more ills you gave rise to.

Damian had lost his lung back in the old days, before the Warming. It happened when a neighbourhood plant making videotape polluted the air. The plant, naturally, had been neutroned and the resultant destruction shown on neighbourhood noticeboards and peasant laptops across the planet. But that had been a long time ago. The pictures had faded from the screens and Brighton lay like Atlantis beneath the warm North Sea.

And he had found himself, at twenty, unemployable. So, after taking a three-day course at the television centre,

Damian had been despatched as a cost-estimator to a Theatre of Deprivation.

In Middle Africa, in a crescent stretching thousands of kilometres from coast to coast, a vast area depopulated by the viral epidemics, Damian travelled, calculating the amount of maize permitted per head, building airfields for the food drops. Travelling by train. Attended by the usual staff. The frontier was tough. He suffered continually from Monitor's neck, the results of weeks in the field spent studying reports on the VCR. His train once struck and killed several indigenes. Official videos fired into those villages by the Protection Forces had made it clear that it was only by staying there that some, at least, would survive the shortages. It seemed to Damian that they preferred to die beneath his wheels but of course it would have been quite incorrect to have said so. And Damian valued his job.

Ruby-Louise ran the food trains, the big transports winging out of the west with grain and drugs and administrators for the imploded countries run by the Health and Security agencies. He liked Ruby-Louise and she liked him. So they made an agreement.

When they returned from the other world, from the Theatres of Deprivation, people were, quite naturally, suspicious. Ruby-Louise had been out there for a long time. Who could say what she was carrying? She'd been very good about this. She wore her gloves whenever she left the house and was happy to retreat into the sterile bubble whenever friends came to dinner. It did little good to tell people that she'd been screened on her return from the other world and shown to be acceptable. Nowadays people were immensely virally aware. You simply felt you had to support their right to personal anxiety even if science said you were as clean as a whistle.

Then came the trauma. Her GP appeared on the screen one night and said he'd had a call from the Geneological Office.

It seemed that Ruby-Louise's maternal background showed unacceptable risk. He strongly advised a pre-emptive strike. Ruby-Louise cried and said she wouldn't do it. But the firm young face on the screen reminded her that if she chose to ignore the figures, and the disease struck, she might be refused treatment in much the way, long ago, smokers, drinkers, cholesterol addicts, the overweight, the undersized, and those found to carry the gene for violence, were routinely turned aside as being deemed to have brought their misfortunes upon themselves.

So Ruby-Louise had pre-emptive breast surgery and all had been fine for about ten years when her GP reminded her that she was now over seventy and that every succeeding year her chances of being struck by the family probability increased markedly. Better safe than sorry. Leave it too long and it could be dicey.

So Ruby-Louise decided to have the other off.

And that should have been that. But a few days later the mail box bleeped and postal announcements told Ruby-Louise her GGP had something he wanted to share with her.

The face on the screen was as smooth and as white as one of those ancient clock faces you sometimes saw in very old videos of very old churches before they all fell down. The General Gene Practitioner had looked at her LEG rating. Ruby-Louise was of course free to ask what her cut-off prediction was. She was a little over seventy and the average life-expectancy grade for women was about 136. Men still trailed at about 125. No one knew why; though the latest best guess in the clinic said it was related to falling sperm count. Ruby-Louise said, after much reflection, that she did not want to know her LEG, because they only ever revised these things downwards.

'Say I am to go at little more than a hundred, or even younger – at ninety something. Do I want to know? Damian, I do not.'

One day Damian came home to find his dinner in the microwave and a note from Ruby-Louise:

Heat on Mark 5 for 30 seconds. Have taken the day out.
Love R-L
PS Do not over-cook.

That had been nearly twenty years ago. Now he was on his day out. He needed the break. But he couldn't remember why he needed a break. He'd tried every enhancer on the market. But his memory grew worse. He kept his forgetfulness to himself. He signed up to one of the biggest memory banks on offer. He never strayed without a modem so he could access the facts he needed – in case someone asked him.

It was so bad he could not even remember when they had shot the poets. He could remember what the poets had said before they shot them – that they were advertising writers, or underwriters, or ships' writers and public relations officers and priests and ordinary people who never harmed anybody. But it hadn't helped – they shot them. And Damian could not remember why.

When his vehicle suddenly slowed he thought he must have lost power for some reason. It was only when the window opened and the squeaky voice demanded to know why it'd been picking up oscillations in the vehicle that Damian realised that he might be in some trouble.

'I was singing,' he said carefully.

That the police officer found this unsatisfactory was clear from the twinkling line of lights that glowed between its plastic brows. 'LMSB' Damian caught himself thinking. And immediately felt ashamed of himself for this petty computerism. Large Memory, Small Brain – that's what they said about them.

The police officer looked Damian over. Grey eyes like icy pools – and then asked his destination. Police officers' voices were designed to deter. This one sounded like he'd OD'd on nitrous oxide. Damian said he was on his way to the Day Centre.

The officer began checking the vehicle's instruments, the voice recorder, the alcohol monitor, the anti-nicotine screener. Taking readings from the navigational computer. Checking the transponder points. Why had Damian loaded his smart card with only enough credit for a one-way trip?

Eventually the officer ordered him in its high voice to stop unnecessary vocal oscillations within the vehicle. It reminded him that single trips, to whatever destination, were forbidden. And to deliberately set out on a journey without sufficient credit to return was an offence.

Damian said he felt that there were exceptions. A day out, for instance. The officer replied that there were no exceptions.

The first he saw of the Centre was a strawberry neon sign on the roof. 'Camp Sunrise Welcomes One and All.' He imagined a simple, pleasant little ceremony. The couch, a cup of tea and a biscuit, a smile from the nurse, the slight discomfort of the needle, and away you went.

That's how he had always thought of Ruby-Louise's day out. Telling the nurse cheerfully that she was 'genetically privileged' and how she had lost one breast and then the other because that's what her genotype said she should do. Ah, yes. Ruby-Louise had been the closest thing he knew to an old-fashioned patriot. They had mapped her genotype and Ruby-Louise had played by the map. My genotype, right or wrong.

It was nightfall before he got inside. A revolving workstation in a striped apron was hosing out a giant fridge. It was evidently one of those dual jobs, programmed for cleaning and consolation. It sniffed, testing whether he was organic; it depended for readings on its sensitive sniffer nose. Identifying him from his breath as 'human, elderly, lungless, slight liver damage', it went into religious mode. 'Go home, now, my son,' it advised, in warm brown vowels. Then it fitted a nozzle into its mouth and began sucking the ash out of the ovens.

Damian sat down at an empty table. Someone had left a pile of glasses and a dozen beer bottles on the table. A geranium wilted in a pink plastic tub. Remnants of some happy family's away-day. Friends had come along to wave them goodbye.

He repeated that he was on his day out.

'Get yourself a private scheme, my son,' said the work-station. 'Save yourself a lot of grief.'

The cleaner/consoler opened the door and pointed him into the dark. Where had he been living for the past few decades? New York? Entitlements be blowed. Those days were dead and gone. Something for nothing days. Camp Sunrise took emergencies only. And there were waiting lists for those. Sufficient need – you had to prove need. Stretcher cases took priority. Even then there were lengthy delays. Blockages in the fridge, stoppages in the ovens. The machines were old. They needed investment. The authorities preferred to target specific groups. Groups in need.

'Tomorrow,' said the workstation, 'have a good day,' and closed the door in his face.

Damian stood in the dark. All his tomorrows stretched ahead – as far into the future as he could see. Except he could see nothing. Where was his day out? He'd always believed in a decent conclusion. A friendly finish. Now the end began to look as if it had not even begun.

The Ice Warrior

David Hartnett

David Hartnett read English at Exeter College, Oxford. His collections of poems include HOUSE OF MOON and DARK AGES. BLACK MILK, a novel, was published in 1994. He is currently working on a second novel, a collection of short stories and a fourth collection of poems.

THE ICE WARRIOR was read by Frances Jeater, and broadcast on Radio 4.

The Ice Warrior

It had begun snowing again, fat flakes slanting past the apartment's plate-glass windows then spiralling down to the resort in the valley below. Although it was only five o'clock in the afternoon, dusk seeped over everything. On the hillock opposite, clumps of spruce and fir withdrew into their white shrouds. Where the resort opened out into a complex of rinks and playgrounds, the lake lay muffled and sluggish. On green slimed rafts, their wattled heads tucked under wings, Muscovy ducks balanced one-legged, like iced carvings of themselves.

'Spring snow. They say it's the best for ski-ing.'

There was no answer. Turning from the window she slumped into the nearest armchair.

'You'll want to ski yourself.'

Again no one replied and she reached for the remote control on the table. There was a soft crackle as the television in the corner came alive in a blizzard of pixels. Tilting the remote control, she pressed one channel button randomly after another: the news in Italian, Benny Hill dubbed into German. She sighed again and closed her eyes.

Slim, with bobbed greying hair and the ghost of a dimple in the middle of her left cheek, Maud Pelling looked young for her fifty-two years. She wore black padded ski-pants and a fine light blue cashmere jersey, its left breast pinned with a silver half-moon brooch which she fingered now and then, caressingly. Nothing in dress or gesture suggested that, on this day, ten years ago, her husband had disappeared for ever.

Opening her eyes again she let them wander round the room. She had bought this apartment a year after her husband's vanishing. It did duty, in her mind, for the memorial which Peter's continuing absence seemed both to require yet forbid. In earlier days, they had often talked of buying a holiday home in the Alps: both for themselves and their only son Michael, who had already shown an interest in wintersports. Now, every Easter, she and Michael came out from Sussex to Switzerland for a fortnight's holiday. Together, for what they both referred to as 'the anniversary', they strove to conceal the abyss into which Peter had so suddenly plunged.

This Easter, though, was to be different. Her son would not come out until the second week. He had broken the news during her last visit to see him up at Oxford, mentioning his old tutor's 'absolutely crucial' dig down on Salisbury Plain. Her fingers sought the half moon brooch again. That had been his peace offering, a salving of guilt for not accompanying her when she set out from the house in Hove to fly here. He knew she hated travelling abroad by herself. It was at such times she bitterly missed her husband.

She remembered the night before the disappearance. Peter had been quite normal, if a little high, after his flight back to England from clinching the Hong Kong deal. Nursing a tumbler of Scotch he had let her show him the new curtains in the dining-room. She remembered how he had brushed back the blond quiff from his forehead and leant forward (a tall man as his son would be), peering with myopic exaggeration.

Then next morning he had become that other being: a negative of himself, a missing person. She had not suspected at first, even when he was late home from work. But a phone call from his partner had revealed his daylong absence. Soon panic set in. He was wandering somewhere, dazed by amnesia, or lying, blue with hypothermia, up on the Downs. The police turned up the company car in a multi-storey near Gatwick and evidence of a one night stopover in the Hilton. Anxiety gave way to euphoria. He was neither dead nor injured. He would return. But as day merged into day and Peter neither returned nor made contact, a numbness set in, punctuated by flashes of anger and guilt. Even death, she felt, was preferable to this lack of explanation.

In front of her the TV snowed on, a programme whose sequence of frames changed second by second. How quickly the images came and went, each tantalising yet ungraspable: a man in a cloak, then the mouth of a cave, toothed with icicles, then a child shovelling snow to build a snowman. Frozen yet sucked forward, she struggled to understand the flux on the screen. Michael's brooch fell under the armchair, its pin loosened by her fingering. She began to cry.

The gin slid into a chilled, cloudy tumbler. She dabbed at eyes and nose. Tonic foamed and the ice cubes cracked. She had been wrong to feel so upset. Michael would soon fly out to join her. After a period of boyish dismay and grief he had coped with his father's strange vanishing, fighting the darkness like his mother. He would make a historian everybody said, perhaps an archaeologist. Despite his blond hair and gangly physique, the son was different from the father. Walking back to her chair, she paused at the sideboard to scan the letter he had sent from the dig in Wiltshire: 'The site was probably occupied into the early Bronze Age. We've turned up a number of axe heads. None of them local. From the Alps mostly.'

The second gin worked its dull, uplifting alchemy. The third lulled an already weakened appetite and handed her over to a happier past, before Peter's disappearance. They were driving through Switzerland. Michael was six. They had been toying with the idea of a holiday apartment even then. It was late summer. Head-scarved women bent with scythes on a quilt of tiny pastures. Behind the braided yellow netting of electric fences, dark-eyed cattle peered over precipices, their leather-strapped bells clanging in muffled unison. Peter was talking: 'This was one of the last areas in Europe to be opened up to civilisation.'

He paused to change gear, then went on: 'Further up this valley there was a village that could only be reached by ladders. They used to pull them up every night. Imagine that. Completely isolated. As if you didn't exist.'

Michael was strapped into the back seat. He had slept on the long haul over the Simplon Pass but was awake now and playing vigorously with his vast collection of plastic warriors: space heroes, troglodytic demons and, most treasured because most recently acquired, an ice warrior. According to the legend on the box this particular figure could melt at will, disappearing behind his mirror-like shield. Blond-haired and impossibly muscled he carried a spear and an axe. Yet despite his strength and weaponry, the ice warrior had fallen easy prey to a trap set by his plastic enemies. He lay now upside down in a crevasse between the seat and the armrest. His fate had been sealed by a woeful moral weakness. He was – as Michael chanted over and over again – naughty, nasty and naughty.

The meadows and the villages were behind them now.

Climbing through a series of sharp hairpin bends the road drew them into a bluer cooler world. She shivered and wound up her window. Soon they came to a level plateau. Sheets of early snow lay here and there, melting at the edges into rock. The road straightened and suddenly they were at the mouth of a long valley. At its far end between two serrated peaks, a greyish cliff hung like a curtain. Peter's words echoed across the years: 'It's the source of the Rhone. The glacier.'

Beside the road, still more stream than river, the Rhone gushed clear and fast over polished stones. The face of the cliff was deeply striated and wrinkled. From fissures here and there, torrents of water spouted.

'Look Michael, a glacier.'

Their son thrust his head out of the window – he already had his belt unbuckled in anticipation of a stop – and waved the ice warrior aloft. The thunder of the cascades almost obliterated her next remark.

'And look, a turnstile. You can go inside it. Into the glacier.'

The tunnel wound back into the cliff. Its walls were blue and dripping. It was cold in the tunnel too, so that she had to stop to button up Michael's anorak. Suddenly he wriggled free and ran dragging his fist along the glowing azure walls

'Don't do that Michael. You'll soak your glove.'

'It's not me, it's him.'

He held up the plastic figure. Its body was caked with ice.

The tunnel ended in a cell hollowed out of the ice. Before them stood a man balancing a camera on a tripod. Another man strode forward. He was dressed in a shaggy polar bear suit, the bear head tucked under his crooked arm. They wanted to take a picture. Before she could protest the bear had replaced his head and wrapped his paw round Michael's shoulder. She turned to enlist Peter's aid. And found he was gone. Michael was giggling into the ice-tagged fur of the man-bear.

'Watch him. He can turn into a ghost.'

The photographer didn't understand but laughed anyway. The camera flash blinded her for a second.

She found Peter in the car park on the far side of the pay kiosk. His face was in shadow, as he explained how he had wanted to see the glacier, not be roped into a tourist trap. He sounded slightly shamefaced.

'Well we were roped in anyway.'

She held up the still sticky Polaroid of herself, Michael and the bear. The ice warrior appeared too. Suddenly Michael began to whimper.

'My warrior, my warrior.'

He had left it behind in the tunnel. So she went back, paying for a second time, past the man in the bear suit taking a breather at the entrance, a cigarette peeping from a mouth packed with ursine teeth, then through the blue tunnel and on into the photographer's lair. Her German hadn't been so good in those days. The photographer either could not or would not understand. She made a despairing hunt round the glistening walls. Nothing. That night in the hotel in Zurich Michael had crossed to their bed and told them about the hairy man who had taken him inside the mountain.

She still had the Polaroid somewhere.

Something had startled her awake. She looked round blearily. It was dark outside now, the lights in the resort hazed over by the still falling snow. In the corner the TV flickered. She must have pressed the remote control with her foot. She thought she heard a voice:

'He is believed to have begun his journey in one of the valleys on what is now the Italian side of the Alpine range. He evidently knew the routes north but on this fatal trip a combination of bad luck and freak weather sealed his fate. Caught in a spring storm, he began to develop hypothermia. Stumbling on a little way he fell into a crevasse on the glacier and was lost. Time passed. History began. Empires rose and fell. There were wars, migrations, plagues. And through it all the ice warrior slept on, frozen. Then one warm spring day last year glacial melt-water washed out his axe and part of his leather jerkin. A passing mountaineer glimpsed something unusual in the snow. And the rest as they say is history.'

The screen showed a shrivelled figure on a laboratory slab. She leaned forward, listening:

'He was a warrior and a trader. Axes like the one he carried have been found as far north as Wiltshire. In Zurich . . .'

It was very late. Swaying upright, she released the strings of the bamboo blinds with a clatter. The TV screen died into itself.

Later that night Maud Pelling was woken for a second time. The sound on this occasion was barely a voice, more a kind of crying: high-pitched, insistent, as though she were being summoned by a creature half animal, half child. She stood up, wrapping a dressing-gown round aching shoulders and lurched unsteadily along the dark white corridor towards the apartment's front door.

When he held out the plastic figurine she took it without protest. She knew he had travelled a long way to return it to her. The figure was wet and cold. An ice crystal lay unmelted on its torso. Shield and axe had gone. She looked up. He was older than she remembered. But still blond, still tall. He swayed slightly, this almost transparent man with the ripped leather coat and the mountaineer's crampon. Now he was leaning towards her, as if to speak. Afterwards she remembered the blue gash in his forehead.

It had stopped snowing. The mountains glowed pink in the morning light. Snow quilted trees and rooftops. She drained the soapy glass of soluble aspirin and looked down into the valley. There was a faint mist on the lake. The Muscovies moved across its bright surface. Early skaters on the ice rink cried their high-pitched self-absorbed cries. She turned from the window, smiling.

Heroin Man

Tom Drury

Tom Drury was born in 1956 in Mason City, Iowa. His first novel, THE END OF VANDALISM, was published in 1994. He is a *New Yorker* contributor and lives in Connecticut with family and pets. He is now at work on a second novel.

THE HEROIN MAN was first broadcast on Radio 4.

Heroin Man

Frost drove an oil truck in Vermont, a big orange oil truck, through the Green Mountains. Sometimes he thought his customers were like junkies. They would call him in the middle of the night: 'We're out, Frost. We're bone dry. We hate to bother you but you gotta come over and give us some. I'm sorry Frost, but we're shivering. We won't make it till morning, buddy.'

Sometimes Frost for the fun of it would mentally substitute the word heroin for the word oil during conversations with his customers.

'Say, we were wondering if we couldn't have our heroin delivered at a certain time each month, instead of having to call you in a major panic when we run out.'

'Sure we can do that.'

'The thing is I'm not sure how much heroin we use. Probably quite a lot. Grandma's home all day and she really likes to crank it up.'

Frost would not have been engaging in such pointless comparisons had it not been October already and had Frost not been restless all year. The contented mind is not driven to make similes. The contented mind is aware of the individuality of each thing.

Frost was about to turn forty-four. He had a wife and four children. The children were named Nate, Julia, Wedge, and Candy, and they fought all the time. Their hatred was a thing of wonder, and yet Frost knew it was common. Once he had gone to a therapist who said, 'I can understand this ambivalence about your siblings, Rick. I myself am an only child but you see I have two children of my own and sometimes it seems as though they really, truly cannot stand one another.'

'My kids are, oh, what's the word, like cherubs,' said Frost. And they were, then. It was only later, when there were more of them, that they turned evil.

The therapist was on Frost's oil route. He was the sort who liked to come out and stand around while the oil was running, as if Frost was going to steal the drain pipes off his house. On the other hand the therapist worked at home and didn't have many customers. Where Frost lived a lot of people had businesses in their homes and Frost always hesitated to go in. He didn't want to use the wrong door or interrupt a squalid family scene. The therapist would smile sentimentally as if receiving communion instead of heating oil. Another simile – you can have it.

Frost went home at the end of another day. He pulled up the driveway, parked the orange truck, and went inside. Wedge and Candy were insulting each other deftly while carefully watching cartoons and sitting with perfect composure in armchairs.

'Everyone hates you.'

'Shut up.'

'Make me.'

'I don't make trash, I burn it.'

'If you died everyone would sing Hallelujah.'

'If you died everyone would dance around the Maypole.'

'That's enough,' said Frost. 'If one of you died the other

would feel terrible guilt for years. So unless you want to fritter your lives away in a series of depressions, I'd advise you both to pipe down right now.'

But Wedge had to push it. 'If Candy died all the birds would burst forth in glorious song.'

'I'll turn that TV off,' said Frost, 'if that's what it takes.'

Upstairs Nate, Julia, and Frost's wife, Deirdre, were in the family room watching *Walt Disney's Fantasia* on the video player. That's how they always said it around the Frost household, Disney's name included, a measure of respect for the man whose impact on America rivalled that of Jesus or Thomas Paine. It was the part of *Fantasia* when the Hieronymus Bosch ghouls have returned to the graveyard after a night of terror and 'Ave Maria' is playing and people are walking over a bridge with lanterns in the early light. Deirdre was holding on to a big glass of Seagram's and Coke and sobbing silently.

'It's just so sad,' she said. 'I mean, it's all right there, isn't it? The viciousness of life but, yes, its beauty. Look, Rick, the people are coming home . . .'

'I like this part too,' said Frost. He lowered himself into a beanbag chair to watch and immediately began wondering how he would manage to get up again. 'How was work?' said Frost.

'Terrible,' said Deirdre, who was a bus dispatcher. 'One of the drivers, Bob Smith, ran over these two ladies who were crossing the street without a care in the world.'

'What do you mean, ran over? You're exaggerating, aren't you? I'm sure he didn't run them over.'

'Oh but he did.'

Frost looked at Deirdre but her eyes were locked on to the screen. 'So they're, what, dead? Two dead ladies, and Bob Smith sitting in jail on a murder rap.'

'One has a possible leg fracture, that tells you something.'

'It tells me he didn't run over them.'

She glared at him. 'Yes! He ran over their legs! What am I talking for, my own enjoyment?'

'You never said a word about legs,' said Frost. 'You implied these women were crushed. All right? That's what run over means to any rational person.'

'You know, I must say, we were very happily watching *Walt Disney's Fantasia*, until you strolled in.'

'I can't get up,' said Frost. 'So you're going to have to learn to live with me.'

'How was your work?' said Deirdre.

'Do you know Virginia Lasalle?' said Frost.

'Yes.'

'That Lasalle couple living up on Caspian Avenue.'

'Right.'

'So I'm hooking up the hose and Virginia comes out of the house and she says, "Say, I know this isn't really your line of work, but my car won't start, and I wonder if you have any ideas." So I say, "Well, did you look under the hood?" And she says, "What would I be looking *for*?" So we go over and she gets behind the wheel of their Plymouth Fury and I lift the hood and what do you think she's got in there? Rabbits. And I say, "When was the last time you had this car running?" And she says, "Yesterday." And I say, "Mrs Lasalle, I hate to disagree, but I don't think it was yesterday." So she says, "Well, one of those days." She says, "Since my husband took off I have no way of getting to the dentist."'

'I didn't know the Lasalles were split up,' said Deirdre. 'But it makes me sick the way people take advantage of you. They want you to do everything but deliver oil.'

'Let's have a taste of that drink,' said Frost.

'Now don't get too comfortable down there, because don't forget, we have that carnival to go to.'

'I did forget. What is that about?' said Frost.

'It's the regular carnival that comes every year for

Oktoberfest,' said Deirdre. 'Part of the proceeds are going to my book club this year.'

'We don't have an Oktoberfest.'

'Look, I don't know what you call it. This is October, isn't it. Call it what you like.'

'That shoddy carnival?'

'You call it such.'

Deirdre's book club was taking over the town. Everywhere Frost looked he saw people carrying the same books, like religious zombies. One week they read *Metamorphoses* by Ovid, and Frost opened Deirdre's copy and read the line: 'The fire supplied what light there was – how useful!' He liked this so much he borrowed it. At work just the other day his supervisor said, 'Joey Robinson got the flu so you and Cochrane have to split up his route,' and Frost said, 'How useful.'

Deirdre had liked the Ovid book because women cried in it and turned into plants.

'One thing I don't get,' said Frost, 'is why a book club needs to raise money. Reading is still free, isn't it?'

'For refreshments,' said Deirdre.

The carnival was held in the park in the Frosts' town beside the new-age playgrounds, which were made of lumber and tyres and resembled a prison for medieval children. The kids fought in the back of the station wagon and Nate elbowed Julia in the solar plexus. Julia gasped several times for air and then slumped forward.

'Oh God, Rick, pull over,' said Deirdre. 'Oh my baby.'

Frost stopped the car and gently lifted Julia back to a sitting position. 'Well, this is a first,' he said to Nate. 'You've knocked her out cold. Hey, Julia. Hey, little one.'

'Come back, Julia,' said Nate. He took his sister's hand. 'Please come back.'

Julia's face was pale. Frost, Deirdre, and Nate were kind of marvelling at how pretty she was in this inert state, when gradually her eyelids fluttered up, revealing her baby blues. 'I've been far away from you,' she said. 'I had arthroscopic surgery but now I'm OK.'

Wedge and Candy were crying fearfully in the most remote part of the station wagon. 'Do we still get to ride the circus wheel?' said Candy.

The carnival had no ferris wheel. The only ride was a specious contraption consisting of metal chairs suspended by chains from a dozen overhead spokes that turned on a rusted hub.

'No way you're getting on that,' said Frost. 'I'm sorry. No I think not. Too dangerous.'

'Rides are supposed to be dangerous,' said Wedge.

'To create the illusion of danger,' said Frost. 'Big difference. We just had a scare with your sister passing out on account of Nate, and I don't really want to push our luck.'

All the sideshow attractions were in the backs of trucks, so that everyone spent the night climbing like movers in and out of semi-trailers. There were two monkeys in a cage. They were called Adam and Eve and their eyes were deep and startling. The children gave them peanuts.

'They look so grievous it almost seems like they could talk,' said Deirdre. 'Isn't that strange? I wonder how old they are. They look like they're getting up there. I wonder what they would say if only they could speak.'

'Probably something along the lines of, "For the love of God, open the cage,"' said Frost. 'I would think escape would be uppermost on their minds.'

'I wish they wouldn't look at us that way,' said Deirdre. 'It's not like we did anything.'

'Look at them,' said Frost. 'They've seen it all a thousand times. Every town like the one before. Next! That's what they're saying. Next!'

'Let's move on,' said Deirdre. 'Let's go see the Mummy's Hand. Come on children. Don't tease the monkeys. Julia, do not hurl the peanut. Gently toss, gently toss the peanut.'

In the Big Top a sharpshooter picked off tiny green buttons on a white board propped against an easel. A woman named Cleo arranged the buttons with sinuous gestures. She had a great figure.

'You see what's happening, don't you?' said Frost.

Deirdre was trying to sneak passages from the big paperback she was supposed to have done in two days. 'The man is shooting,' she murmured.

'Sure he is,' said Frost. 'And the targets are falling. So we assume he's hitting the targets. But what if he's only hitting the board? The board would not be hard to hit. In fact the *board* would be hard to miss.'

'I think the assistant is doing something,' said Deirdre. 'She has strings attached to her fingers. Mark my words.'

'Strings?' said Frost. 'You have lost it.'

They could not agree what was happening and talked about it all the way home and even after the kids were asleep. 'Strings,' said Frost, before turning out the light. 'Strings, right.'

The phone rang after midnight. Frost was out of bed simultaneously with the sound. The phone was in the hallway.

'Frost, you gave me too much,' said Mrs Lasalle.

'Too much what,' said Frost.

'In my basement. Oil. It ran over.' There was a muffled sound on the line and it almost sounded like she was laughing. 'I've been smelling something all night. Finally I had the presence of mind to check.'

'A lot or a little? Can you see the pool? Is it bigger than a large braided rug? Do you have a service contract?'

'Smaller than a rug, I would say. But, let's face it, any oil is too much.'

'I'll be over,' said Frost.

Mrs Lasalle had a bad gasket on her oil tank. Frost replaced it and cleaned up the oil that had spilled. He had to write a report for the state and so afterwards he took notes at Mrs Lasalle's kitchen table.

'Thank you for coming out,' she said. She stood up and got some pills down from the top of the refrigerator. 'I'm having some work done on my teeth and they gave me these for the pain. Take one. You always seem to be carrying around the weight of the world. This will change your outlook.'

Frost looked at her in the dim light. His eyes felt large and dry. 'Mrs Lasalle, I don't know if that's good or bad.'

She smiled. 'Oh, it's good, all right,' she said. 'It's like lying by a stream with the wind blowing in the grass. That's the closest thing I know.'

Frost got a glass of water and took the pill. 'I could use some of that,' he said.

The Pillow Goose

Jane Gardam

Jane Gardam has written many novels and short stories. She is a Whitbread Award winner; and GOD ON THE ROCKS was shortlisted for the Booker Prize and also made into a film for television. Her recent books include THE IRON COAST about Teesside, and a story collection GOING INTO A DARK HOUSE. A new novel will be published later this year. She lives in East Kent for some of the year and also in the Yorkshire Dales.

THE PILLOW GOOSE was first broadcast on Radio 4.

The Pillow Goose

There were two sisters, Maude and Angela, who lived on the Thanet marshes in a cottage left them by their great-grandmother. They were craft workers in metals, wool and cloth and dried flowering things, and they were as green as grass.

They would eat no meat nor anything from a dairy and their shoes were made of plastic and they fainted at the sight of furs. They took all their bottles and jars and waste paper to the tip every Sunday morning at eight o'clock prompt, like Communion, and put everything carefully down the right holes.

The sisters had no husbands but many lovers, and because they did not believe in contraception except by the phases of the moon there were many babies born in the cottage over the years, and these all grew up and went away. And the sisters took life lightly as the leaves grow on the tree and as they grew older sang as happily as ever at the loom and forge and dyeing-tub, bashing out the metals for their quaint and fairly unsaleable jewellery, eating home-made bread, baked more or less evenly, in their twig-burning stove, washing their long and beautiful hair in the purest non-animal soaps or with some of their great-grandmother's herbal mixtures and drying it under the flowering trees of their little orchard.

When lovers had grown scarce and their hair was becoming grey there came one day to the cottage the most enchanting Ethiopian gypsy, and the sisters were happy. When he left them after several days, secretly one morning at dawn, they found on the rough old kitchen table propped up with a log, the gift of a sort of hay-box and inside it two beautiful goose eggs. Maude and Angela wept at the gypsy's going, laughed at the strange present and shoved it under the table. They went on with their work, each with her own sweet thoughts about the gypsy's visit.

Out from the eggs hatched two untidy-looking goslings and the sisters looked up in one of their great-grandmother's useful books in the garret some rules about rearing them. They installed them in an old hen house where they became magnificent white geese.

Quite soon there were more eggs which in turn became scruffy goslings and then more white geese. The sisters grew to love all the geese and the flock grew. In no time at all there was a great gaggle of the most dazzling and noble birds moving with stately tread in little troupes among the cherry trees, beaks left, beaks right, cackle, cackle, cackle. They seemed whiter and more perfect than any known geese. Had each worn on the top of its silken head a miniature crown like in the ballet *Swan Lake* you would only have thought, 'How very appropriate'.

Word went round, as it does, about these geese in the Thanet marshes. Somehow they became known as 'The Ethiopian Royal Geese', and of course everyone knows that Ethiopian pillow down has been treasured for a millennium at least. One small bolster will cost you hundreds of pounds. The heads of royalty have lain on such things since Tamburlaine came crashing through Asia. King Arthur gave them as prizes for knightly behaviour all round the round table, and the Pharaohs were provided with stacks of them in the Pyramids to comfort them in the next world.

Dreams that arise from such pillows are most disturbing and delicious, and the sisters who had always been poor came to understand that they were now in charge of a fortune.

But they did not believe in the slaughter of animals. And geese, ever famous for clearing up rubbish, for their comic beauty, for their filthy temper, and for saving Rome are best of all known as creatures for the pot and for delicious horrors like pâté de foie gras. And the plucking of the famous down, so light and soft that it seems caught from the very air, like clouds of dandelion fluff, down that has to be escorted to the pillow-makers by special messengers armed with machine guns and mortars to places of special safety – this down can only be obtained after the goose is dead.

Now the sisters were not too frightened about owning the miraculous brood for it is hard to steal geese. They are as fearsome as the rhinoceros and faster, and they have powers that can tell the approach of a robber at half a mile. What the sisters did grow cross about as the flock grew were the endless visits of the pillow-makers of the world to discuss lucrative deals. They were also troubled by the enormous fecundity of the geese who were now standing shoulder to shoulder (if geese had shoulders) in the orchard, and soon spread across the little garden, tight as the Royal Enclosure at Ascot, in the heavily fenced paddock. Every shed, the rickety barn, the old earth closet, the tumbledown cow-house long unused, the coal-hole, the wood-store and at length the scullery, the parlour and the spare bedroom were filled with geese; and from the air the land surrounding the cottage looked as if it were in the grip of a deep localised snowstorm. The raucous music of the geese could be heard far across the marshes disturbing the slumbers of sailors out in the English Channel. The smell of the geese and the depth of their excreta (which even in the Ethiopian Royal Pillow Goose resembles bundles of large rotting cigars) was causing concern to workers in the gentler fumes of the Richborough power station. In Canterbury Cathedral the clergy were wearing face masks for Evensong. Animal rights groups were vociferous about the over-crowded conditions and although the sisters were paid-up card-carrying members of these organisations they were spared nothing by their own kind who now stood round the cottage chanting and waving banners.

The girls would not sell or give away any of the geese of course, for how can you ever trust anyone not to make an easy, if blood-stained, fortune?

So there had to be a way found to limit the breeding powers of the geese without contraception and for their down to be painlessly plucked without their death; and this seemed quite impossible until one day Maude thought of using the idea of temporary anaesthetic before plucking, and then the creatures might be wrapped in warm coats until their feathers grew again.

Maude and Angela presented themselves then to various distinguished veterinarians of the day who were each and all unsympathetic to their ideas. Next they sat in the cottage in deep thought until Angela said, 'Perhaps our great-grandmother who was known for herbal simples might be of some help.'

So they ransacked the shelves in the garret again and came upon a bottle thick with cobwebs labelled 'For the temporary sterilisation and anaesthetising of geese for the purpose of de-downing.'

Then Maude and Angela set about making a woollen garment like a baby's romper suit with holes for legs and slits for wings and aperture facilities for private and egg laying parts, and good strong press-studs down the breast and along the undercarriage. They knitted hundreds of these suits in strong white wool, then scattered about half the contents of the cobwebby bottle in the goose mash. There was an old, old faded label on the bottle, but no directions about the strength of the contents that turned out to be a thick, bluish-black liquid like an old peculiar treacle.

The next morning every goose in the goosery was lying on its back with its great yellow feet in the air and its black eyes shut. The sisters took them two by two and with several friends of their own ilk (and not prone to sneezing) they settled themselves in the parlour of the cottage and plucked all day and all night. Gently they lifted the geese from the goose sheds and the coal hole and the barn and the outside loo and the scullery and the spare bedroom and gently they replaced them, all wrapped in their comfortable knitting. From a distance they still looked just like white geese.

And in the cottage the pluckers sat for all the world as if they were out of the world; inside a luminous airy summer cloud.

Now the sisters had to wait and see. About luncheon time the feet of the geese began to twitch, the necks of the geese began to turn this way and that in their usual stiff way. The fierce black eyes of the geese began to open and the outraged, ill-tempered, arrogant gobble of the geese began to gobble.

And Maude and Angela went to London in a hired van and sold the down for a fortune, keeping back just enough for a pillow each for themselves. Most of the fortune they immediately gave away to good causes. It is said that no finer goose down has even been known in the history of the world.

The sisters now looked after the geese very kindly. They seemed happy in their knitted coats; perfectly well and perhaps pleased at their rest from egg-laying. Some died, but only in the natural way of things, and from old age. A fox got one – its knitted coat, two webbed feet and a beak were found beside the boundary fence and this saddened the sisters and they tried hard not to rejoice when the fox was found lying dead with a blue-black tinge on its face: for all animals only act according to their nature and death comes to us all.

What was more troubling was that the white woollen coats of the geese were beginning to grow filthy. They had sagged or shrunk with the weather, become covered with burs and prickles and twigs and the geese had begun to pull and tear at them with their beaks and to stand about in silent humiliation.

One morning Maude came in from taking the geese their mash, puzzled.

'Come and see,' she said.

'What?' asked Angela.

'Do you not see something strange?'

Angela looked at the flock in their dirty woollies under the polished fruits of the cherry trees. She said, 'They seem to be faintly coloured somehow, under the wool.'

They had a go at catching some of the geese to see what was going on beneath, but they would have none of it. They hissed and spat and lunged at Maude and Angela. Their eyes were sad and wild.

The sisters then ransacked the garret to see if there were any bottles to do with the re-habilitation of un-downed geese, but there were none. They tried again to read the label of the cobwebby bottle. No go. And the bottle now was empty. The blue treacle had vanished.

Maude and Angela were distraught. The geese had begun to look, quite suddenly very decrepit, like dirty toddlers trailing woollen rompers. They fixed the sisters with dae-monic stares and would not let them near. They began to wilt and pine and sink to the ground like little heaps of washing. At the gate of the cottage the animal rights people chanted, and about the world the pillow-makers wouldn't cease their clamouring for more down.

Then a boy came knocking at the door, a dark boy with sparkling eyes and a cross face who said his name was Scratch.

'I think I know you,' said Angela.

'You should do,' he said, 'I'm your son.'

'Darling,' said Angela, 'My own.'

'Angel', said Maude, 'My treasure.'

'I don't know which of you I belong to,' said Scratch, 'I never did. It was a messy life this place but I suppose I love you and your high notions and I've come to save you' and he sat all night up a tree in the orchard playing his flute. (He had to sit up a tree because the grass was disgusting.) And all through the night hours the geese listened and grew calm, and Angela and Maude sat in the parlour trying to remember details of old times: there must some years ago have been another, musical Ethiopian. And they fell asleep in their chairs.

In the morning the flute was silent and the boy had gone. Tearfully Maude and Angela looked for him. There was a great silence in the goosery, none of the usual clamour of geese getting ready to attack the day. The sisters opened doors and goose flaps and found that during the night the rags of the woollen garments had slipped like the old dull skins of snakes and there streamed across the orchard and paddock a silent flock, all the colours of the rainbow from psychedelic green to the most sinister indigo. The pink ones looked like giant toilet rolls dotted in the sedge.

The press arrived en masse. The cottage made the national news. The RSPCA sent representatives from head office. Many members of the animal rights groups had apoplexy. Local foxes blanched and fled.

Later that day every laying goose in the place dropped a rainbow coloured egg and with the rest of the flock lay down and died. The eggs (except one or two that Scratch had acquired sometime in the dawn and made off with in a little hay box) were all addled from the start and rolled away in the grass of the orchard, where the trees all grew cankers and wilted and fruited no more. The two sisters Angela and Maude packed their bags and disappeared, each with her one down pillow under her arms. It is thought they went to Abyssinia.

It is said that very occasionally a Thanet twitcher on the mud flats has glimpsed a most astonishing bird. It is like a jewel shining on the dun fields, a gleam like a Roman standard blowing among the stones of Richborough Castle where the centurions are said to have first arrived in Britain from Alexandria with the seeds of the pink valerian on their boots. The valerian that still flowers like a weed, a rather crude and ugly pink along the Thanet lanes. But this of course is a ridiculous story.

Unlike the ghostly Rainbow Pillow-Goose of Thanet. This exists all right. It is a wonder and a warning to the world.

The Hero

Joanna Trollope

Joanna Trollope is the author of a number of historical novels and BRITANNIA'S DAUGHTERS, a study of women in the British Empire. She has also written seven contemporary novels, THE CHOIR, A VILLAGE AFFAIR, A PASSIONATE MAN, THE RECTOR'S WIFE, THE MEN AND THE GIRLS, A SPANISH LOVER and THE BEST OF FRIENDS, published in spring 1995.

THE HERO was a co-commission with the *Daily Telegraph* and was broadcast on Radio 4. It was read by Michael Maloney.

∫

The Hero

He stayed on the island much longer than he intended to. This was partly out of indolence and partly to prove all those people wrong – including his mother and his girlfriend – who had said that to decamp to a Mediterranean island for a whole winter to write a novel was both melodramatic and a cliché. He'd get sick of it in weeks, they said. He'd never write a book. He'd be lonely.. Well, he *was* lonely in a way, and he *was* tired of the umbrella pines and the scrub-covered hills and the little port where the same old men sat outside the same old cafés and the same battered boats came in and out. But he had got used to it too, and to the slow rhythm of the days and in any case, his novel was only half done. When he thought about going home, his whole soul shrank from arriving back with only half a novel to show for seven months away with nothing else to do.

So he stayed. The winter – harsh and oddly bleak – wore away to the spring and he planted basil and geraniums on his tiny balcony and idled about in front of his typewriter. In the evenings, he went down to the harbour front and sat in one bar or another and read the local newspaper and joined in conversations about the weather or the fishing catch or the Mayor of the little port who had won on a Communist ticket, but who lived like a capitalist with a Mercedes and a villa with a swimming pool and a new wife who dressed like a harlot.

'It was different,' someone said one night, offering him one of the pungent local cigarettes, full of black tobacco, 'when we had the English Mayor. Quite different. He was a gentleman.'

He stopped lighting the cigarette and put it down.

'English? An English Mayor? Here?'

'Yes,' the old man said. He raised a hand. 'In 1944. I remember him well. He was military governor.' He paused for emphasis. 'He was a hero.'

Several other men nearby stopped talking and moved closer.

'It's true,' one said, 'my father knew him.'

'He's buried here,' the old man said. 'Didn't you know?'

He shook his head.

'I never heard of him— '

'You should have,' the old man said reprovingly. 'You an Englishman and you don't know of Captain Campbell!'

'He's up the hill,' someone else said. 'There are six or seven Protestants up there, in the cemetery beyond the water tower. You'll find him there, with all his medals.'

'And when you've done that,' the old man said, stooping so that he could peer directly into his face, 'you can go and see his widow.'

'His widow— '

'Yes, yes, his widow! Are you deaf? She is an islander, she lives here, in the port, with her memories. She will tell you how it was when Captain Campbell was the hero of this island!'

He woke next morning to a day of perfect spring, clear and blue and polished. It was a Tuesday, the day on which the weekly letter from his girlfriend usually lay waiting for him at the post office. He decided, with a mixture of relief and guilt, that he was in no hurry to collect it today, chiefly because, for the first time in months, he had something other, and more pressing, to do. So he draped a towel over his typewriter to smother its reproaches and set off up the steep streets to the cemetery high above the port where the Protestants had been safely segregated in death, away from the Catholic faithful.

It was a tiny plot, surrounded by tumbledown walls and full of tough winter weeds. There were half a dozen headstones, most at crazy angles, but only one looked tended. The ground around it had been roughly cleared and a red geranium had been planted in a white plastic pot. The lettering on the stone was simple. 'Edward Archibald Campbell' it read, '1895–1957. D.S.O. Croix de Guerre.'

He looked at it for a long time and then at the earth under which Edward Campbell, husband, hero, and military governor, lay. Then, in a burst of sudden gratitude, he knelt for a moment, and closed his eyes. Below his knees lay not just a man, but a story.

Signora Campbell was not at all surprised to see him.

'People come,' she said. 'People often come. To talk about my husband.'

Her villa was small and dark and crammed with furniture. It smelled of cats. Signora Campbell herself looked exactly like any other elderly islander, stout and dressed in black with grey hair held back in a bun with combs.

'But I was pretty once,' she said.

She showed him photographs of herself in 1944, proudly leaning against a tall, smiling man in uniform.

'That was Edward. He was very handsome.'

He said, 'Can you tell me about him?'

'He was a hero of the French Resistance,' she said, as if

declaiming it. 'He helped British airmen who had baled out over occupied France to escape to England. The British gave him the DSO. The French,' she paused for dramatic effect, 'awarded him the Croix de Guerre.'

He peered about him in the gloom.

'Of course you have his medals— '

'No,' she said proudly. 'No. He was too modest to keep them. But I have this.'

She moved across the room and indicated a framed letter on the wall, a huge flamboyant, illuminated thing.

'From the people of the port,' she said, 'in grateful thanks. In humble thanks. Are you a journalist?'

'No,' he said, 'a writer.'

'Then to you I will entrust this.'

She went across the room to an ornate bureau and unlocked the topmost drawer. From it, she took a big, faded folder, tied up in pink lawyer's tape.

'His autobiography,' she said reverently. 'His own, true story. You must read it tonight and return it to me without fail tomorrow morning.'

He read all night. He couldn't stop. The style was crude and boyish but the story was spell-binding. Edward Campbell, youngest son of a small town Scottish doctor and educated by the Jesuits, had survived as a pilot with the Royal Flying Corps in the First World War. In the Second World War he had been recalled to buy transport in France for the British Expeditionary Force in 1940 and, though overrun by the Germans, had eluded capture to become the vital organiser in the escape and evasion operation. After internment in Spain – on monstrously trumped-up charges – he had ended up as regional governor of the island, restoring order to a grateful civilian population after the chaos left behind by the retreating Axis. He concluded the book in Somerset. 'I sit here to write the final page in the land I love, the land it has been my sole desire to serve.' It was *Boys' Own Paper* stuff and it was wonderful.

In the morning, he went back to Signora Campbell and begged to be allowed to borrow the manuscript for two weeks.

'Just a fortnight. I promise I'll return it. But there's someone I want to show it to. Someone in London. It's an amazing story.'

She made him sign a receipt with his English address as well as his address on the island. She was solemn when she shook his hand goodbye.

'You must be very trustworthy. You are taking my treasure.'

'Of course,' he said. He was much moved.

He kept the folder with him all the flight home, lying on his knees like a baby. Sometimes he would open it and take out a page, and the bold, smiling, nonchalant personality of Edward Campbell would rise up before him, as palpable as if he occupied the next airline seat. It was a story in a hundred thousand, a story to make not just a book but a film, an international film, with the final credits – including his own name as screenwriter – moving slowly over a last lingering shot of that simple, noble headstone among the weeds on a Mediterranean island.

'Marvellous,' his agent said, 'a terrific story.'

He waited. His agent always reacted like this at first. It was the things he said next you had to listen to.

'A real boys' book. Plenty of action. Of course— '

'Yes?'

'We have to verify all this.'

'But I saw the grave . . .'

'Yes. But all the same. It won't be difficult, you know. He must be the star of half the books on the occupation of France and the French Embassy will know all about him. And the Ministry of Defence. Go and do a couple of days scouting about and I'll get this copied meanwhile. This could be a real spinner, you know. It really could.'

The assistant Military Attaché at the French Embassy was apologetic: 'You see, we have no record of Captain Campbell. But sometimes, in war the Croix de Guerre was awarded in the field and never reached official records. Perhaps you could find more details from the British records? I am so sorry . . .'

The Army Records Office kept him waiting twenty minutes in a ferociously clean room painted shiny cream. He was conducted, at last, into an office where a man stood, half-smiling, behind a desk with his hand held out.

'Do excuse me for keeping you waiting. I was in a meeting, you see, but wanted to see you myself. Do sit down.'

He looked at the fat file on the man's desk. It seemed to contain, among other things, a manuscript.

'Captain Campbell, I believe. That's who you're after? I feel bound to tell you, I'm afraid, that you're not the first.'

He sat down abruptly, his eyes still fixed on the file.

'What do you mean?'

The man laid his hand on the file, almost affectionately.

'Terrific fellow. I've become quite fond of him over the years. But I'm afraid the whole thing's a fantasy. He was just a charming adventurer, with the gift of the gab— '

'But the honours!' he cried out. 'The DSO! The Croix de Guerre!'

'He invented them. He invented at least three-quarters of his life. It's an awful disappointment, I know. I felt it myself, when I first discovered. If it's any comfort to you, I've come to see that he believed it all himself in the end, every imaginary, boastful word of it.'

*   *   *

He went back to the island two days later, cradling the manuscript as carefully as he had done on the outward journey. He had felt in awe of it then; now he only felt protective, as if Edward Campbell must be shielded from the truth about himself as much as the island and the widow must be. He had no idea what he would say to the widow in actual words and phrases. All he knew was that he felt above all else that she must never know what he now knew. She and the island must keep their hero safe. It was his duty to make sure that they could.

He took a taxi from the airport straight to Signora Campbell's villa. She opened the door to him with an air of expectancy and, as if to add some mark of celebration, he saw she had added a string of amber beads to her stout black frock.

'Well?' she said.

He looked at her. Her eyes were bright. He was convulsed with the determination not to let her down.

He said slowly, to emphasise how much he was in earnest, 'I – decided it wasn't a story for the world. I'm so sorry. But it belongs here, you see. I've become convinced that it's a story for the island.'

'Quite so,' she said.

She reached out and almost snatched the folder from him, pressing it against her bosom. Her voice was exultant. 'Quite so.'

Negatives

E. Annie Proulx

E. Annie Proulx's first story collection was HEARTSONGS AND OTHER STORIES, followed by a novel, POSTCARDS, which won the 1993 PEN/Faulkner Award for Fiction. Her second novel, THE SHIPPING NEWS won the *Chicago Tribune's* Heartland Prize, the Pulitzer Prize and the *Irish Times* International Fiction Prize. She is at present writing another novel, THE ACCORDION CRIMES. She lives in Vermont and Newfoundland.

NEGATIVES was first broadcast on Radio 3, and read by William Hootkins.

$\int$

Negatives

Year after year rich people moved into the mountains and built glass houses at high elevations; at sunset when the valleys were smothered in leathery shadow, the heliodor mansions flashed like an armada signalling for the attack. The newest of these eyries belonged to Buck B., a forcibly retired television personality attracted to scenery. A crew of outside carpenters arrived in the fall and laboured until spring. Trucks bearing great sheets of tempered glass crept over the dirt roads. The owner stayed scarce until June when his dusty Mercedes, with an inverted bicycle on the roof, pulled up at the village store and in came Buck B. clenching a map and asking for directions to his own house.

A few weeks later, the first yellow cab ever seen in the town disgorged Walter Welter in the same place. Walter, who had come a long way in ten years from Coma, Texas, called Buck B. on the pay phone, said he was at the store and Buck B. could just get down there and pick him up. The cab driver bought a can of pineapple juice and a generic cheese sandwich, waited in his taxi.

'I give 'em a year,' said the storekeeper peering out

between advertising placards, watching Walter transfer tripods, portfolios, cameras and six suitcases from the taxi to the Mercedes.

'Tell you what *I'd* give 'em,' said the tough customer. 'What *I'd* do.'

But it all was all over before the first snow and no one had to do a thing.

'Why do you let that slut come here?' said Buck, casting his lightless eyes on Walter who knelt beside the tub in the downstairs bathroom. Buck's hands were crusted with clay, held stiff in front of his black apron. Walter's hands were in yellow rubber gloves, scrubbing away Albina Muth's greasy ring. Buck's face was all chops and long teeth like the face of Fernandel in old French comedies; his hair rippled like silver water.

'You think you're going to get some photographs, don't you? That she's some kind of a subject. The Rural Downtrodden. And then what, the pictures lie around in stacks. Nobody but you knows what they are. The edge of an ear. A dirty foot. You better keep her out of the upstairs.' He waited but Walter said nothing. After ten or eleven seconds Buck kicked the bathroom door shut, stalked back to his clay, hands held in front of him like ceremonial knives shaped for cutting out viscera.

The fingers on both hands wouldn't count the dinners Walter Welter ruined with his stories of Albina Muth. Friends came up from the city for a mountain weekend, had to listen to grisly accounts: she had left her awful husband for a deranged survivalist who hid knives under tin cans in the woods; she lived with an elderly curtain-rod salesman made such a satyr by rural retirement that Albina had been rushed twice to the emergency room; she was being prosecuted for welfare fraud; her children had headlice; she sported a vestigial tail.

They saw her at the mall supermarket standing in line with children clustered on the cart like flies, or carrying bags of beer and potato chips out to a pickup truck in the parking lot. Her children, with thick-lidded eyes and reptilian mouths, sat in the bark-strewn truck bed rolling empty soda cans. Albina, her hair squashed against her head, climbed into the passenger seat of the cab, smoked cigarettes, waiting for someone who would come later.

One day Walter passed her walking on the muddy shoulder of the road, the children stumbling and squalling behind her. He pulled up, asked if she wanted a ride.

'Sure as hell do.' Smoky, rough voice. She stuffed the kids with their chapped, smeared faces, into the back seat and got in beside him. She was thin, about the size of a twelve-year-old. Her coarse hair looked like she cut it herself with a jackknife, her white face like a folded slice of store bread. He noticed, not the colour of her eyes, but the bruised-looking flesh around them.

'Know where the Bullgut Road is? Next one after that's my road. You'n drop us there.' The tone was bold. She bit at her nails, spitting fragments off the tip of her tongue.

The road was a skidder-gouged track. She pulled the half-asleep children out like sacks, saying 'Come on, come on,' and started up through the mud, one brat jammed on to her hip, the other two coming at their own pace and crying. He waved, but she didn't look around.

At dinner Walter did an imitation of the way she wiped her nose on the back of her hand. Buck B. listened, tarnished hair clouded with clay dust, eating his dish of yogurt and nuts, gazing through the glass wall at the mountain. He said, 'God, that's beautiful. Why don't you do mountain studies? Why don't you take pictures of something attractive?' Then he said he was afraid that Albina Muth's children had sowed the back seat of the

Mercedes with louse nits. They were starting to fight when the phone rang and Walter got the last word, saying, 'I'm not here if it's one of your stupid friends wanting a tree picture.' He meant Barb Cigar who once had called to say that her trees were covered with lovely perfect leaves and didn't Walter want to come with his camera? No, he did not. It was Barb Cigar with the dew-lapped mouth like the flews of a hound who had given Buck B. an antique sabre reputed to have fallen from Casimir Pulaski's hand in the battle for Savannah (a parting token from her ex-father-in-law from his cutlery collection), she who had sent a youth in a panda bear suit to sing Happy Birthday under Buck's window, she who named her Rottweiler puppy 'Mr B'.

Walter Welter's photographs were choked down and spare, out-of-focus, the horizons tilted, unrecognisable objects looming in the foreground, the heads of people quartered and halved. What he called the best one showed a small, boxy house with a grape arbour and a porch glider. The grass needed cutting. Guests sorting through the photographs kept coming back to this dull scene until gradually the image of the house showed its secret hostility, the arbour turned harsh and offensive, the heavy grass bent with rage. The strength of the photograph emerged as though the viewer's eye was itself a developing medium. It would happen a lot faster, said Buck, if Walter wrote out the caption: *The House where Ernest and Lora Cool were Bludgeoned by their Son, Buxton Cool*.

'If you have to say what something's about,' said Walter, 'it's not about anything except you saying it's about something.'

'Spare me,' said Buck, 'spare me these deep philosophical insights.'

*   *   *

Walter's photographer friends sent him prints: an arrangement of goat intestines on back-lit glass, a dead wallaby in a waterhole, a man – chin up – swallowing a squid tentacle coming out of a burning escalator, Muslim women swathed in curtains of blood. One of the friends called from Toronto, said he'd spent the summer with the archaeologists flying over the north looking for tent rings. 'There was this Inuit cache on the Boothia Peninsula.' Distance twisted his voice into a thinning ribbon.

The wooden box, he said, fell apart when it was lifted from the earth. Inside they had found knives, scrapers, two intact phonograph records of religious music, a bullet mould, a pair of cracked spectacles, a cooking pot stamped *Reo*, needles, a tobacco can. From the tobacco can they took a dozen negatives, the emulsion cracked with age. Prints were on the way to Walter.

When they arrived he was disappointed. All but one of the photographs showed squinting missionaries. The other photograph was of an Inuit child in front of a weather-whitened building. Her anorak was sewn in a pattern of chevrons and in the crazed distance lay a masted ship. Her face had the shape of a hazelnut, the eyebrows curved like willow leaves. She leaned against the scarred clapboards, arms folded over her breast, mouth set in a pinched smile and both eyes lost in their sockets.

Walter caught the flaw in the shadow. Light coursed through the space between the soles of the child's boots and the ground because her weight was on her heels. She was propped against the building.

'It's a corpse,' said Walter, delighted. 'She's stiff.'

Buck, toasting oatcakes, wondered what the photograph meant. 'Like Nanook of the North, maybe? Starved to death? Or tuberculosis? Something like that?'

Walter said there was no point in trying to understand what it meant. 'It can't mean anything to us. It only meant something to the one who put this negative in the tobacco can.'

Buck, wearing a scratchy wool sweater next to his skin, said something under his breath.

Once or twice a week they drove to the mall with its chain stores, pizza stands, liquor store, sixty-minute photo shop, While-U-Wait optician, House of Shoes, bargain carpet, and Universal Herbals.

'I told you to bring the other credit card,' said Buck. 'I told you the Visa was ruined when it fell under the seat and you moved it back.'

Walter pawed through his pockets. He leapt when Albina Muth rapped on the passenger window with a beer bottle. She was smiling, leaning out of a garbage truck parked beside them, smoke flooding out of her mouth, her rough brown hair like fur. She was wearing the same grimy, stretched-out acrylic sweater.

'Nice truck,' cried Walter. 'Big.'

'It ain't mine. It's a friend of mine's. I'm just waitin' for him.' She glanced across the highway where there were three low-slung bars: the 74, the Horseshoe, Skippy's.

Walter joked with her. In the driver's seat Buck invisibly knotted up, yanked himself into a swarm of feelings. He had found the other credit card in his own pocket. Albina threw back her head to swallow beer and Walter noticed the grainy rings of dirt on her throat.

'You take pictures?'

'Yeah.'

'Well, sometime maybe you'n take one of me?'

'For god's sake,' hissed Buck, 'let's go.'

But Walter did want to photograph her, the way she had looked that day by the side of the road, the light strong and flickering.

*   *   *

In October Albina Muth started to sleep in the Mercedes. Walter went out on Sunday to get the papers. There she was, so cold she couldn't sit up. He had to pull her upright. Dull, black-circled eyes, shivering fits. She couldn't say what she was doing there. He guessed it was a case of Saturday night drinking and fighting, run off and hide in somebody's car. It was a two-mile walk from the main road to somebody's Mercedes and all in the dark.

He brought her into the house. The south wall, glass from roof to ground, framed the mountain, an ascending mass of rock in dull strokes of rose madder, brown tongues of fume twisting out of the springs on its flanks. The mountain pressed into the room with an insinuation of augury. Flashing particles of ice dust stippled the air around the house. The wind shook the walls and liquid shuddered in the glass.

In that meaningful house Albina Muth was terrible, pallid face marked by the weave of the automobile upholstery, hands like roots, and stinking ragbag clothes. She followed Walter into the kitchen where Buck worked a mathematical puzzle and drank seaweed tea, his lowered eyelids as smooth as porcelain, one bare monk's foot tapping air.

'What?' he said, shooting up like an umbrella, jangling the cup, slopping the puzzle page. He limped from the room, the cast on his right foot tapping.

'What happened to him?' said Albina. She was attracted to sores.

Walter poured coffee. 'He hit a deer.'

'Didn't hurt the car none!'

'He wasn't in the car. He was riding his bicycle.'

Albina laughed through a mouthful of coffee. 'Hit a deer ridin' a bike!'

'The deer stood there and he thought it would run off so he kept on going but it didn't and he hit it. Then the deer did run off and Buck had a broken ankle and a wrecked bike.'

She wiped her mouth, looked around. 'This is some place,' she said. 'Not yours, though. His.'

'Yeah.'

'Must be rich.'

'He used to be on television. Long ago. Back in the long ago. A kids' show – *Mr B.'s Playhouse*. Before you were born. Now he makes pottery. That's one of his cups you're drinking from. That bowl with the apples.'

She put her head on one side and looked at the table, the clay floor tiles, the cast-iron bulldog, the hand-carved cactus coat rack, drank the coffee with a noise like a drain and over the rim of the blue cup she winked at Walter.

'He's rich,' she said. 'Can I take a bath?'

What would she say, thought Walter, if she saw Buck B.'s bathroom upstairs with the François Lalanne tub in the shape of a blue hippopotamus? He showed her to the downstairs bath.

She came many times after that, walking up the private road in the dark, crawling into the car and filling it with her stale breath. Walter threw a sleeping bag in the back seat. She added a plastic trash bag stuffed with sweaters and wrinkled polyester slacks, a matted hairbrush, pair of pink plastic shoes with a butterfly design punched over the toe. He wondered what she had done with her children but didn't ask.

In the mornings she waited outside the kitchen door until Walter let her in. He watched her dunk toast crusts, listened to her circular talk that collapsed inward as a seashell narrows and twists upon itself, and at noon when the bars opened he took her to the mall.

'Come on, take my picture. Nobody never took my picture since I was a kid,' she said.

'Someday.'

'Walter, she is living in my car,' said Buck B. He could barely speak.

Walter threw him a high smile.

The deep autumn came quickly. Abandoned cats and dogs skulked along the roads. The flare of leaves died, the mountain moulted into grey-brown like a dull bird. A mood of destruction erupted when a bull got loose at the cattle auction house and trampled an elderly farmer, when a car was forced off the road by pimpled troublemakers throwing pumpkins. Hunters came for the deer and blood trickled along their truck fenders. Walter took pictures of them leaning against their pickups. Through binoculars Buck watched loggers clearcut the mountain's slope, and Albina Muth slept in the Mercedes every night.

Walter liked the road called Mud Pitch and drove past the wreck of the old poorhouse two or three times a week. This time it showed itself to him like some kind of grainy Russian nude tinted egg-yolk yellow. As he stared the sunlight failed and once more it became a ruined building. He thought he would photograph the place. Tomorrow. Or the day after.

A cold front rolled in while they slept and in the morning the light jangled through cracking clouds, the sky between the house and the mountain filled with loops of wind. The camera strap sawed into the side of Walter's neck as he ran down the terraces to the car. He could hear the bulldozers on the mountain. Albina Muth was curled up on the back seat.

'I'm working today. Got to drop you off early.'

The mountain mottled and darkened under cloud shadow. There was no colour in the fields, only a few deep scribbles of madder and chalky biscuit. Albina sat up, face thickened with sleep.

'I'nt bother you. Just lay here in the car. I'm sick.'

'Look. I'm going to be working all day. The car will be cold.'

'Can't go back up to the trailer, see? Can't go to the mall. He's there, see?'

'Don't tell me anything about it.' He cut the Mercedes too far back, put the rear wheels in Buck's spider lily beds. 'Don't tell me about your fights.'

The poorhouse was a rack of wind-scraped buildings in fitful sunlight, glaring and then dark like the stuttering end of a reel of film spitting out numbers and raw light. Albina followed him through the burdocks.

'I thought you wanted to stay in the car and sleep.'

'Oh, I'n look around.'

Inside the rooms were as small as pantries and closets. Furrows of clay-coloured plaster had fallen away from the lath, glass spindled across the floor. The stairs were slides of rubbish, bottles, feathers, rags.

'You gonna fix this place up?' she said kicking nut husks, pulling light chains connected to burst bulbs.

'I'm taking pictures,' said Walter.

'Hey, take my picture, OK?'

He ignored her, went into a room: punched-out door panels, drifts of flies in the corners and the paint cracked like dried mud. He heard her in another room, scratching in the filth.

'Come in here. Stand by the window,' he called. He was astonished by the complexity of light in the small chamber; a wave of abrasive grey fell in from the window, faded and deepened along the wall with the swell and heave of damp plaster. She put her arm along the top of the low window, embracing the paintless frame and resting her head on her shoulder.

'Just like that.'

The light flattened so she appeared part of the window casing.

'For god's sake take that disgusting sweater off.'

Her knowing smirk disappeared into the hollow of the rising sweater. She thought she knew what they were about. Her mouth ruched, she stood on alternate feet and kicked off her pants. She was all vertical, downward line, narrow arms and legs like wood strips, one nipple blank, erased by light, the other a tiny gleam in the meagre shadow of her body. She waited for Walter to bite her arms or shove her against the soiled wall. He ordered her to move around the room.

'Now by the door – put your hand on the doorknob.'

Her purpled fingers half-closed on the china globe. The dumb flesh took the light from the window, she coughed, leaned against the door and the paint fell in brittle flakes. But there was a doggishness about her bent shoulders, her knuckled back, that goaded him.

'Behind the door. Squeeze into that broken panel. Don't smile.'

Her face appeared in the splintered opening, washed with the false importance the camera inflicts. *Click . . . whirr*

Walter's thrusting look swept the room across the hall; he saw on the floor a mound of broken glass, splinters and curved blades sloped in a truncated cone. Light pierced a broken shutter.

'Squat down over that pile of glass.' A hot feeling rushed through him. It was going to be a tremendous image. He knew it.

'Jesus, I could get cut.'

'You won't. Just keep your balance.'

Submissively she lowered herself over the glass, the tense, bitten fingers touching the dirty floor for balance. Spots of sunlight flew across her face and neck as the clouds twitched along. She filled the viewfinder.

Again the angled limbs, the hairy shadows and glimmering flexures of her body.

'Can I put my clothes on? I'm freezin'.'

'Not yet. A few more.'

'Must of taken a hunderd,' she cried.

'Come on.'

She followed along to the end of the poorhouse where green shelves pulled away, to the fallen door that led like a ramp into the world. He headed for an old kitchen stove with a water reservoir, rusting in the weeds. The oven door fell away when he grasped the handle. Albina hung back, contracted and shivering.

'Albina, pretend you're crawling into the oven.'

'I want to git my clothes on.'

'Right after this one. This is the last one.'

'I'n wait for you in the car.'

'Albina. You pestered me over and over to take your picture. Now I'm taking it. Come on, crawl into the oven.'

She came through the weeds and bent before the iron hole. Her hands, her head and shoulders went into the stove's interior.

'Get in as far as you can.'

The blackened, curved soles of her feet, the taut buttocks and hams, the furred pinch of sex appeared in the view-finder. There was no vestigial tail. She began to back out as he worked the shutter.

'I wanted you to take pictures of me smilin',' she said. 'Thought they was goin' to be cute, I could get like a little gold frame. Or maybe like sexy, I could put them in a little black fold-up. Not gettin' in no stove, behind stickin' out.'

'Albina, honey, they are cute, and some are sexy. Just a few more. Come on, stand in the hot water thing on the side there.'

She climbed up onto the stove top, saying something he couldn't hear, stepped into the water reservoir. In a cloud of rust her feet plunged through the rotten metal. The top of the range was even with her waist, and she looked as though she were to be immolated in some terrible rite. Blood ran down her foot.

Helpless, dirty laughter spurted out of the corners of his mouth and Albina wept and cursed him. But yes, now he could squeeze that hard, thin thigh, pinch the nipples until she gasped. He thrust her against the stove. Later, when he dropped her at the bar, he gave her two twenties, told her not to sleep in the car any more. She said nothing, stuffed the money in her purse and got out, walked away, the plastic bag of clothes bumping against her leg.

Milky light spilled out of the house. Buck's shadow was limping back and forth, bending down, lifting, its shape distorted by runnelling moisture on the windows. Walter went in through the side door, down the back stairs to the basement darkroom.

The film creaked as he wound it on to the reel. He shook the developing tank, stood in the sour dark listening to the slip and fall of water, watching the radiant hand of the clock. The listless water slid away, he turned on the light. Upstairs Buck walked back and forth. Walter squinted at the wet negatives, at the white pinched eyes and burning lips, the black flesh with its vacant shadows, yes, a thin arm crooked down, splayed fingers and the cone of glass that looked like smouldering coals. He really had something this time. He went upstairs.

Buck stood against the wall, hands behind his back. On his good foot he wore a brown oxford with a thick sole. There were all of Walter's suitcases at the door.

'It's getting too cold,' Buck B. said, voice like a ratchet clicking through the stops.

'Too cold?'

'Too cold for staying here. I'm closing the house up. Tonight. Now.' He had another house in Boca Raton but Walter had never seen it.

'I thought we were going to stay for the snow.'

'I'm selling it. I've put it on the market.'

'Look, I've got negatives drying. What am I supposed to do?' He tried to keep his voice level in contrast to Buck's which was skidding.

'Do whatever you want. But do it somewhere else. Go see Albina Muth.'

'Look— '

'I'm sick and tired of having a tenant in my car. The Mercedes actually smells, it stinks, or haven't you noticed? The car is ruined. I'm sick and tired of listening to Albina Muth suck up my coffee. And I'm tired of you. In fact, you can have the car, the stinking car you ruined. Get in it and get out. Now.'

'Look, this is ironic. Albina Muth is not coming back. She took all her stuff out of the car. This was it. Today. I took some pictures and that was it.'

Buck B. looked toward the black window, toward the mountain drowned in the canyon of night, still seeing the slope stripped of trees, strewn with rammel and broken slash, and beyond this newly cleared slope another hill and the field with the poorhouse visible for the first time through the binoculars.

'Get out,' he said through his nose, limping forward and raising Barb Cigar's ex-father-in-law's sabre. 'Get out.'

Walter almost laughed, old Buck B. with his red face and waving a Polish sabre. The Mercedes wasn't a bad consolation prize. He could have the interior steam-cleaned or deodorised or something. All he had to do was run back down the stairs, get the negatives and exit, this way out, one way to the Mercedes. He tried it.

The Humming

Michèle Roberts

Michèle Roberts is a poet and novelist. She is half French and lives in London and in France. Her sixth book DAUGHTERS OF THE HOUSE was shortlisted for the Booker Prize and won the WH Smith Award. Her most recent work is FLESH AND BLOOD and she is now at work on a new novel.

THE HUMMING was broadcast on Radio 4, and read by Gillian Bevan.

The Humming

It began with the voices, the sound of muttering that pressed up against the back of her neck, as though the voices were hands that grasped and stroked her, raising gooseflesh. After a little, the voices ceased quarrelling and sank away to a whisper, to be replaced by an unnerving solo, a thin, high, wavering humming, that went on and on, until Clothilde sat up in the darkness and cried out and the unearthly humming stopped.

She knew that the farmhouse was supposedly haunted. The notary who showed them the place and sold it to them mentioned, with a sniff, something about peasant prejudices. Their new neighbours further up the hill recounted the tale with relish, over glasses of kir and sweet fortified wine and dishes of salted crackers. The postman advised Clothilde to put a statue of the Virgin in the empty niche over the front door, as protection. The lady in the bakery cocked her head on one side every morning when they went in for the bread, as though waiting to hear news of hideous apparitions.

Clothilde and Fernande repeated to everyone who offered

them these rumours, these hints and shrugs and winks: we don't believe in ghosts.

Of course the house had character, or as Fernande put it: atmosphere. She was the more romantic and sensitive one, with a nose for such things. She had fallen in love with the house at first sight, a jumble of ancient buildings around a courtyard set in isolation halfway up the hillside outside the village of Sainte Gemme-les-fleuves backed by woods and looped about with streams and tiny waterfalls. While the notary conscientiously pointed out the holes in the roof, the faulty wiring, the lack of septic tank, the dilapidation of barns and outhouses, and the possibility of ghosts, Fernande saw the vine growing spreadeagled against the back wall, the tidy vegetable plot edged with pinks and daisies, the big kitchen's vaulted ceiling and stone-flagged floor, the carvings around the arch framing the huge front doorway. She sat on the doorstep, half in and half out of the house, looking out of the courtyard, down the lane into the little valley spread with cornfields and orchards, and felt happiness settle inside her, part of her bones, not to be dislodged. She said to Clothilde who was inspecting the cracked metal lid of the well in the centre of the courtyard: you *must* buy this house.

The notary explained that, centuries before, the farm-house had been part of a convent. The name of the house – Terredieu – God's earth – confirmed that. Nuns in grey habits had sung the Divine Office in what was now the cowshed. Clothilde and Fernande picked their way through the mud into the manure-scented darkness, across a rough floor of combed concrete littered with straw and ancient cowpats. The notary showed them the tower at the back of the house, called the *oubliette*, in which disobedient nuns were locked up on a diet of bread and water. He showed them the long dormitory upstairs, where the nuns had slept, now become a grainstore, its corners silted with corn husks, and the huge kitchen-living-room, and the tumbledown traces of the cloister around the courtyard. Flinching, he opened the door of the privy and let them peer in. Finally, with a contemptuous smile, he mentioned the local people's belief that the house was haunted.

'Oh do tell us the story,' Fernande implored, ignoring Clothilde's frown.

The notary shrugged.

'These stupid peasants will believe anything. It's the usual thing. A nun having a love affair, discovered to be pregnant, so locked up in the *oubliette*. The prioress set her to sewing shrouds as a punishment. She sewed one for herself and one for the baby. But she went mad from being shut up alone for so long. In her sixth month of pregnancy she killed herself and the unborn child. She knotted the shrouds together and hung herself from a hook in the ceiling.'

Clothilde was quite pale, her face glistening with sweat. She said loudly: 'Fernande and I do not believe in ghosts.'

Later on the postman amplified the story.

'It was a double sin, you see, first of all the sin against purity, and then suicide, which is the great sin, the sin against the Holy Ghost. So no wonder her spirit can't rest. Of course all the holy souls in purgatory need our prayers.'

The neighbours up the hill, Parisian art historians enjoying their second home at weekends and enchanted by the quaint folklore of the district, added their own flourish to the tale.

'People say she walks on the night of the full moon, every month, wearing her shroud. You have to bar all the doors and windows against her, so that she can't get in.'

Fernande sighed with relish, curling her long hands, with their red fingernails, around her glass of kir, and admiring her gold ring with its big green tourmaline.

Clothilde snapped: 'As a pharmacist with a rigorous

scientific training I can tell you that ghosts do not exist, except in the imagination of neurotic people probably in need of anti-depressants.'

Her round face was as pink as her silk trouser suit. Fernande changed the subject and began to explain how Clothilde had sold her pharmacy in Le Mans to buy the house here in Sainte Gemme-les-fleuves and how she planned to work as a locum in the district.

'And you yourself, madame?' enquired the neighbours, smiles of greedy curiosity spreading over their faces. 'Will you live here too? You write children's books, you said. Will you be able to do your writing here?'

'Oh, we'll see how it goes,' Fernande said, laughing.

The lady in the bakery added the final flourish.

'The previous owner of the house lives in Alençon. For a long time she let it out to the tenant farmers who were living here. Then she evicted them, because she thought she'd like to do the place up as a holiday home. But after just one month in the house, organising all the local builders and so on to come in and give her estimates for the work, she changed her mind and put the house on the market. That's why you got it so cheap. She wanted to get rid of it as fast as she could.'

'Perhaps she had a guilty conscience,' Fernande suggested. 'Getting rid of her tenants like that, it sounds rather brutal.'

The woman behind the counter lifted two *baguettes* from the rack and handed them over.

'Oh, they don't mind. Not now. They've got used to it. They were due to retire, in any case. They've got a little bungalow three *kilometres* away, near all their children, they're content. They say a modern house with all mod cons is so much pleasanter.'

She nodded her head at Fernande. 'We're all pleased to see the house being properly lived in again.'

She counted out Fernande's change.

'We are tolerant people,' she said, not meeting her customer's eyes. 'We respect one another, you'll find we are all friends here, in the country. We don't make problems for each other.'

Clothilde, who was waiting in the car outside, smiled when these words were recounted to her.

'We must make sure to give them something to talk about, in that case.'

The local people watched the two women settle in to Terredieu. Carloads of visitors were seen to come and go, vans full of furniture arrived, workmen were summoned to dig the septic tank and instal a bathroom. Autumn arrived. Clothilde climbed ladders to clear gutters and mend shutters and replace panes of glass. She was fortifying the house against the approach of winter. In her red jeans and heavy boots she was a sturdy, cheerful figure. She was clearly the masculine one. Fernande, who was more often seen in a skirt, raked up leaves in the orchard and weeded the gravel paths.

In October, in their second month in the house, on the night of the full moon, Clothilde was woken by the sound of voices. Two women muttering, having a quarrel. She sat up in bed. Moonlight drove between the curtains and whitened the floor with its glare, so bright it was disturbing. The voices ricocheted to and fro across the white stripes of moonlight. *You don't really want to, do you? But I do want to, so much.* Clothilde jumped out of bed. She fastened the curtains together with safety pins, so that not a crack opened for the moon to pour streams of silver through. She trembled with cold. The voices fingered the back of her neck and brought her out in goose bumps. She dived back under the duvet, pulled it round her shoulders, buried her face in the pillow, stuck her fingers in her ears. She could not understand why she was alarmed. She said to herself: I am a pharmacist with a rigorous training in science, I do not believe in ghosts.

The mutter of voices trailed away, dissolved into the sounds of the night that Clothilde knew, and recognised as friendly: creaking timbers in the roof as the house settled down, the long hooting of owls hunting in the woods at the top of the hill. She took her fingers out of her ears and relaxed. She thought: I shouldn't have drunk wine at dinner, I've been feeling odd all day, as though I'm coming down with flu, and the wine has upset my digestion, that's all it is. I was imagining things.

Then the humming began. A high-pitched lonely voice shaking itself into the air, a tuneless, eerie sound that went on and on until Clothilde sat up in the darkness, pressed her hands to her cheeks and cried out. The room vibrated as the humming ceased. It seemed to spin, to throw Clothilde forwards, out of bed, up on to her feet. The silence drove her to the door. She clasped the wooden latch in both hands, trembling, feeling sick. She found herself praying, which she had not done since adolescence: Oh God hold me safe in the palm of your hand. Then she burst into tears.

In the morning Fernande exclaimed with concern at Clothilde's pale face and nervous movements, at the dark rings under her eyes, at her shaking hand as she tried to spread apricot jam on a piece of bread.

'I'm all right,' Clothilde snapped. 'I think I'm coming down with a cold, that's all. I didn't sleep too well last night.'

Fernande drained her cup of coffee. She yawned and stretched.

'You're not working today, are you. So why not go back to bed for a bit. Take some aspirin and catch up on some sleep. I'll go into town and do the shopping. Have a rest.'

Clothilde had a bath and put on a clean nightdress. She changed the sheets on her bed, not wanting to return to the

sweat of last night's terror. Sunlight streamed in through
the windows, which she had propped slightly open before
getting in to bed. She could hear pigeons calling to each
other in the depths of the orchard, then the skitter of gravel
as the postman's car dashed up the lane and screeched to a
halt in the yard. She heard him laughing, teasing Fernande
as he handed over one of the airmail letters that arrived
for Clothilde nearly every day, bright with strips of stamps,
a smudged black postmark. Clothilde was delighted at the
thought of her letter. She would save it as a treat for later.
She felt too lazy to go downstairs to collect it, too ashamed
of appearing before the postman in nightdress and negligée.
Dreamily she closed her eyes. She heard him say '. . . the
feast of All Souls . . .' and then his car engine started up and
he was gone, clattering back down the hill over the loose
stones, soon followed by the whine and roar of Fernande's
deux-chevaux as she sped away to do the shopping.

Now the house was quiet. It was hushed and calm, and
full of sun. Clothilde was dozing, half in and half out of
a river of images slipping past in a play of light, floating
under the soft cotton of the duvet smelling of ironing.
The clean pillowcase was cool against her face. She was
swirling down towards deep sleep. She was remembering
that today was the Feast of All Souls, the eve of the Feast of
All Saints, the day when as a child she had always gone with
schoolfriends into church to pray for the souls of the dead
who were reputed to wander abroad on this day begging
for the prayers of the living so that they might be released
finally from purgatory into the bright joys of heaven. The
more churches you visited on All Souls' Day, the more souls,
it was said, you liberated from their torment.

The humming began again. Insistent, pricking at Clothilde's
eyelids, high and thin, pitched between a tune and a
mindless chant. It was the humming sound a person makes
to accompany her sewing. When you have long hems to

stitch, you hum to keep your fingers steadily moving along. Clothilde thought: the ghost has got in, she has got inside somehow. Her fingers, clutched together under the sheet, were lumps of ice. Shivers ran up and down her back, gripped her forehead. She opened her eyes.

A young woman, heavily pregnant, sat cross-legged on the floor in the sunlight, her profile bent over the baby's christening robe to whose hem she was tacking a deep frill of lace. She hummed a high song as she drove her needle in and out. When she lifted her head and turned to stare at Clothilde, she smiled in recognition. She was Clothilde's exact double. She was her mirror image. She winked, then vanished.

'I'm pregnant,' Clothilde said to the spinning room that was full of the new soul released inside her. 'So that's what all this has been about!'

Her baby daughter was born seven and a half months later, much to the joy of her husband who returned from his posting abroad in good time to accompany her to the pre-natal classes. Fernande, who had been such a good friend to her sister during her husband's absence, was delighted to become an aunt, and insisted on standing as godmother. All the neighbours and villagers attended the christening party, and greatly admired the baby's long white christening robe which Clothilde had stitched by hand through the long winter evenings, humming contentedly to herself as she pulled the thread through the fine white cloth.

Final Payments

D. J. Taylor

D. J. Taylor was born in 1960. His books include two novels, GREAT EASTERN LAND (1986) and REAL LIFE (1992), and a critical study, AFTER THE WAR: THE NOVEL AND ENGLAND SINCE 1945 (1993). His new novel, ENGLISH SETTLEMENT, will be published later this year.

FINAL PAYMENTS was read by William Nighy, and first broadcast on Radio 4.

Final Payments

Anyone who's been involved in the game, they'll have a story of how they got started. About how some teacher noticed them in a kickabout at school, some scout picked them out of a youth team game. Some old ex-pro their dad knew; some TV programme about George Best. Even the legends – Charlton, Moore, Hurst – they'll all have their stories. With me it was my dad, which isn't as straightforward as it sounds, really, because my dad wasn't around much when we were kids – he was a traveller in fancy goods, lighters, cigarettes, that sort of thing – and when he was there he was the kind of bloke who goes down the pub instead of sitting in the front room. Still, he saw it, and you have to give him credit for that.

What was even weirder was that at the time – I was thirteen or fourteen maybe – I didn't even like football that much, certainly not with other kids, and if anyone suggested a pick-up game I'd be the first to scoot. But I used to go out to the park sometimes – the old park near the Scrubs that isn't there any more – and kick around, always on my own, with one eye on the path to make sure I could pick up the ball and scarper if anyone else looked as if they wanted to join in. Anyway, I was doing this one time, back in 1975 it would have been, the year Fulham had their cup-run, when I looked up and saw my dad walking towards me over the grass, coming on slowly in that vague way he had, as if he didn't quite know who he was or where he was going. I had the ball on the ground and was sitting on it before you could whistle, but my dad just sort of smiled a bit and carried straight on – he had a way of making you think that whatever you were doing wasn't really important compared to him. But when I got back home that evening he walked into the kitchen where I was having my tea and said, 'Saw you playing down on the park this afternoon didn't I?' Even then, you see, my dad and me didn't get on, so I just nodded, casual like, but waiting to see what would happen next. Then he said, 'You ever play in a team or anything?' It was stupid, when you came to think about it. All those years I'd been doing swimming at school or going on at him to teach me snooker, and now all of a sudden just because he'd seen me playing football he'd come sniffing round to see if there was anything in it for him. I shook my head, but that didn't worry my dad – he knew what I thought about him by this stage – and he just nodded again. But all that week I caught him giving me a glance or two, the sort of glance he'd give women in shops if he thought my mum wasn't looking, and I knew something was up. The thing about my dad was that he had connections – always knew which horse to back, who to go and see if you wanted a car or a sofa on the never-never – so I wasn't surprised when he got me the trial at Rangers. One Friday night after school it was. And I can remember the coach saying when I went up for a high cross and missed it, 'Jesus, I don't suppose he's ever headed a ball in his life.' But I passed it all the same. Typically, my dad didn't turn up – it was fixing he liked, and getting me the trial meant he'd finished his side of the bargain.

Fulham got to the final that year: I watched every game. They had Bobby Moore playing for them – he was getting ready to retire, but he was still good even then – but somehow when they came out of the Wembley tunnel you knew they were never going to beat West Ham.

I'd already played a couple of games in the youth team by then. They'd started me out in defence, but then moved me into midfield on account of my height – I'm five feet seven, which is small for a footballer – but the youth team coach said there'd be no problem about signing schoolboy forms in a year or so. Curiously enough, I wasn't really thinking about it. Plenty of kids down our way fancied themselves as footballers, and you were always hearing about lads who'd signed for Brentford or Chelsea, or turned out for Millwall juniors, but somehow it never came to anything, and a year or so later you'd come across them stacking trolleys in Sainsburys or looking lost in some Sunday League game. The other Rangers apprentices used to talk big sometimes about how they'd make the first team at seventeen, about how there were scouts from the big clubs already looking them over. But I kept my head down, and by '77 or '78 old Lennie the reserve team manager reckoned I was well on my way to making it. You might not be able to do anything about your height, but you can make it work to your advantage, and anywhere around the centre spot the small guy always has it over the six-footer with no pace. I had this trick of shielding the ball as I turned: you had to be a clever centre back to do anything about it.

I can remember the first time I played for the first team: it was the day after my dad finally walked out on us. To be fair it wasn't any big surprise. There'd been women before, all during the time I was a kid – though it always suited my mum not to notice – and then when I was fifteen he'd got this new travelling job with a big confectionery firm in the Midlands, which meant being away from home even more. All the same, I could have done without being told about Carole or Denise or whatever her name was – they'd got a house by this time, somewhere up Wolverhampton way – and my mum in floods of tears the morning before the Leicester game. We won, as it happened, but I didn't remember much about it. I was too busy thinking about my dad standing there in the front room – he was wearing this new suit, and you could see that he really fancied himself in it – and wondering what we were going to do about money. Looking back, I suppose I don't blame my dad that much – he was a good-looking bloke, even in his fifties, and he liked a drink and a talk, which was something my mum was never much interested in – but at the time it was as if he'd stuck two fingers up to the first eighteen years of my life. If I could have got hold of him, I'd have said something like 'All that time when we were kids, if it was so bad why didn't you say so instead of pretending?' If one of your parents makes it clear that they'd sooner not be there, then you start blaming yourself; or them, which is the same thing in a way.

It was November when he left: three months into the season. I was brilliant the rest of that year. Dave Marshall, the old centre half who I'd been brought in to cover for, spent a couple of months in the reserves and then got sold to some non-league outfit because of me. Come April we were in the top six, and we would have got promoted to the Second if we hadn't drawn the last three games. I suppose it was my dad driving me on. There were times, standing by the touchline waiting for a throw-in, mostly, or drifting up through the midfield, when I'd think I saw him in the crowd, turning away, say, behind an advertising hoarding, hidden in the shadow under the roof of the big stand. It's not true that footballers don't see the people watching: I used to think I was stuck in the middle of an enormous room crowded with screaming faces.

We didn't see him again for a while after that. He'd send my mum a postcard – some town in the North where he was stopping overnight – or there'd be a phone call sometimes late at night, but that was all. As far as us kids were concerned, it was as if we didn't exist. When she was fifteen Angie won a dance competition at the Hammersmith Apollo, and we sent him the photograph in the paper and everything, but he never wrote back. After a time, though, I stopped worrying about it. I was nineteen, twenty, playing in the first team every week, there was the odd piece in the *Recorder* about how Spurs were interested in me, and I didn't have to look for company. I'd wonder about the old man sometimes, what it was like in Wolverhampton with Louise or Kay – Carole or Denise was long gone by this time – but it never hit me, like the day it did when he walked out. Meanwhile the family settled down. Angie was doing her nurse's training at the Charing Cross; I was in digs near the ground – I always liked it that you could just see the floodlights out of the upstairs window; the old lady got a council flat Harlesden way. I used to stay over there at weekends, if it wasn't an away game. She had this framed photo of me in that classic footballer's pose – down on one knee, hands crossed over the other one – taken the day I signed on as a pro – on top of the TV, along with the picture of Angie in her dancing gear, old holiday snaps taken in Southend and Clacton.

It was the early '80s by then, and Rangers were still in the Third. Every so often they'd have a run, win half a dozen games in a row, say, and the *Recorder* would run 'Rangers for the top flight?' headlines, but they never fooled me. I knew there wasn't the money, or the interest. The chairman used to go on sometimes about redeveloping the ground and buying in big players, but in the meantime the old wooden stand was falling apart and you could have unloaded the whole defence for a hundred thousand. There were some other bad signs as well. We went through three managers in '82/3, and Jimmy Wood, the only centre forward we'd had who was any good, got sold to Man United for half a million, which was big money in those days.

What with Jimmy going, and the rest of the players not liking it, the cup run took us by surprise. We nearly went out in the first round to a bunch of non-league amateurs from the West Country, and it took a fluky penalty to get us through. But we beat another Third Division side in the second, and then went to Coventry and won 2–1 on an ice-rink in the third. People started looking up after that, and there were a couple of giant-killer pieces in the papers, but even so nobody expected us to make it through the fourth, which was a home tie against Newcastle. Newcastle! It had been Carlisle away the week before. We packed in 17,000 people that day, and scraped home 1–0, with three of ours booked and the Newcastle skipper stretchered off with a broken leg – you could have heard the bone crack south of the river – and the chairman was supposed to have made five grand out of the bookies.

The rest of it was a blur. We played Everton at Goodison in the fifth, and it went to a second replay, but we shaded it 3–2 and I had that kind of warm feeling you get when you know your career's on a roll. I'd been a bit bogged down the last couple of seasons – there'd been a month on loan to Arsenal, but in the end they hadn't wanted me, and a try-out for the Under-21s – but now there were serious blokes in the *Telegraph* and the *Mail* going on about the Rangers midfield powerhouse and its talented playmaker, and the whole team, right down to Vinnie Cousins the reserve team goalkeeper, knew that once it was all over the big clubs would come diving in and nothing old Samuels the chairman could do would stop them.

Funnily enough, the rest of it was a doddle. Some Second Division lot – it might have been Oldham or Port Vale – in the sixth round; 2-0 against Villa in the semi. It was mayhem by then. The papers were full of celebrities going on about how they'd always been Rangers fans – I'd never seen any of them down the ground, and neither had anyone else, and the manager got invited on all the TV sports programmes. But the final looked dodgy: Liverpool. They were ten points clear of the First that year, and they hadn't lost a game in three months. He rang up the day after the semi-final.'It's your dad here' – just like that, as if we'd spoken to each other every week for the last five years. 'Wondered if you could do me a couple of tickets for the final?' Of course I said yes – he was my dad, after all, and I felt I owed it to him – but all the same I wasn't going to make a fuss about it. I just put the tickets in an envelope and sent them off, second class, and forgot about it. But then a week before the final, when it was really just a question of keeping your mind off everything, I went round to see the old lady in Harlesden. I could tell by the way she looked at me when I came through the door that something was up, and sure enough the first thing she said was 'Your dad's been round.' 'Oh yes, and what did he want?' I asked, fairly cold, because I know the old lady can be a soft touch, but she just went on about old times and keeping in contact. He'd come in an Audi Quattro, apparently, so business must have been looking up. It was only when I got up to go that I realised the photo was missing from the top of the TV. According to the old lady – she started crying when I asked her about it – he'd said he wanted 'something to remember me by'.

I was so angry I had to wait until the evening to ring him up. 'Those tickets,' I said, before he could get a word in, 'I want them back. Now.' I think he must have worked out what I was on about, because he tried to make a joke out of it. 'What's that?' he said. 'Not allowed to come and see my own son playing in the Cup Final? 'The tickets,' I said. 'I want them back.' After that it got nasty. 'You can whistle for them,' he said. 'Mandy's looking forward to this, and I promised her we'd go.' I nearly broke the receiver when I put it down.

You'll remember from the papers what happened. We lost 5–1, and never had a chance. All down to the weak midfield, the commentators said, but I wouldn't know. I went down on the bus and stayed in the hotel all right, but I was gone before breakfast. I can remember ending up in a pub in Oxford Street and coming out and hearing someone say that Liverpool had won, but not much else. The queer thing was that I could remember it all: that day knocking the ball about on the old park, my dad walking towards me over the wet grass. But I knew then, knew already, that it was all over. And that I never wanted to kick a ball again.

Away From It All

Frederic Raphael

Frederic Raphael was born in 1931 and educated at Charterhouse and St John's College, Cambridge. His novels include HEAVEN AND EARTH, AFTER THE WAR and A DOUBLE LIFE. He has published four collections of short stories including OXBRIDGE BLUES and most recently THE LATIN LOVER.

AWAY FROM IT ALL was commissioned with *Traveller* magazine and read on Radio 4 by the author.

∫

Away From It All

I have to admit that if it had not been for Milstein, Sylvia and I would never have gone to live in Spain. In 1959, we had two small children and a very small, and unreliable, income. With what money we had, we had bought the short lease of a flat in Highgate on the promise, by the very nice old lady who owned the house, that she would accord us a new, long lease when our present tenancy lapsed. However, when I went upstairs to begin the negotiations which we assumed would lead to our spending the Sixties in Highgate, with our children swinging in Miss Davidson's garden, she told me that, although our children were enchanting and my wife delightful, Mrs Rideout – her diabetic and arthritic sister – had suddenly been widowed and she could not live alone in her condition. She was sorry to disappoint us but she was sure that we would understand; she reminded me, of course, of the comparative thicknesses of blood and water.

The day after being served with this genial eviction order, I had lunch with Milstein at Schmidt's in Charlotte Street. In his black leather blouson, open-necked maroon shirt and reflecting sunglasses, he looked as though he had just rushed in from the Riviera, or was on his way to it. Despite these lineaments of success, he was actually working in Goodge Street as a production assistant. However, even as he sat opposite me, Milstein's busy eyes were touring the room, vigilant for publishers or authors or producers to whom he might render, or threaten, irresistible services.

As we were brought our three courses, for three and sixpence, I tried to supply some new ideas for the break-through British film which we were supposed to be dreaming up together. So far, Milstein's contribution had been to add his name, as co-author and sole producer, to my embryonic script. While I played petulantly with my Schnitzel and complained about Miss Davidson's bourgeois perfidy, Milstein said, 'Look, are you going to eat that red cabbage or not?'

'I'm too worried to eat,' I said. 'I've got a wife, and children, and I don't know where we're going to live.'

'OK if I . . .?' He tilted my red cabbage onto his own unfinished heap. 'I've never understood what you wanted to get married for, anyway.'

I said, 'I don't know that I wanted to get married exactly, but I'm very happy. And we do happen to have children.'

'That's it,' he said, 'isn't it? You're lumbered. You've got a pram in the hall.'

'My problem is not the pram, it's the fact that we very soon won't have a hall.'

'Leave it with me,' Milstein said.

'The pram?'

'The problem.' He spent agitated seconds consuming the red cabbage. 'Because . . .' I remained passive as he forked the last of my Schnitzel. 'Because . . .' He thrust some bread into his mouth and was waving the basket for a supplementary supply. 'Because . . . all right, here's an idea: how do you feel about Spain?'

'We shall have to get rid of Franco,' I said, 'and introduce a democratic system which more or less restores the Republic, and then . . .'

'Yeah, yeah,' Milstein said, 'but I meant how do you feel about living there for a bit? Great place to work.'

'Spain? I can't go to Spain . . . I've got . . .'

'Only I happen to know this bint— '

'This *what*?'

'Bint, I know this bint, this woman, she's got a house in Southern Spain and, out of season, you can have it for nuppence a month. There's a maid, there's sunshine, there's the sea: everything you want.'

'Spain is a Fascist state,' I said.

'That's why it's so cheap. She'll love it; she can have servants, she can get a suntan, she'll love it. Place called Fuengirola this house is in.'

'Who is *she*?'

'Your wife. Sylvia. It's a fishing village. You can finish our film.'

'I'd sooner write a novel.'

'Finish our film – do you want the *strudel* or the ice cream? – and then you can write all the novels you like. Tell you what, if you're not hungry, order the ice cream, I'll have the *strudel* and then I can . . .'

I said, 'Who is this "bint" of yours?'

'Cynthia's not mine, well, not any more: she's Henry Cake's now.'

'Henry Cake?'

'Henry Cake, Henry Cake! The brilliant new Hackney playwright, works with Joan, lives with Cyn. Don't you know *anyone*? How soon can you be ready to travel?'

'I can't even afford to get to Spain.'

'Yes, you can,' Milstein said. 'Look, are you going to finish that beer or not?'

A week later, Sylvia and I were loading our children and all our possessions into and on to our green Ford Anglia,

PLD 75, and began the long and often pot-holed journey to Fuengirola. Cynthia Langham's cottage was small and neat and you looked over the patio wall at the empty beach and the unpolluted Mediterranean. Salvadora cooked our meals and cleaned and taught us her sibilant-free Andalusian Spanish in which *España* itself became '*Eppaña*'.

My new novel put on weight with marvellous speed. At weekends, we visited Ronda and Coín and Malaga and Granada and Cordoba. Liberated from Harold Macmillan's senescent England, we discovered the joys of a world elsewhere. We made new friends, writers and painters and Mutual Funds salesmen who came from New York and Miami and Paris and Ibiza. None of them had heard of Henry Cake.

We had been in Cynthia's house for just over a month when I got a CALL IMMEDIATELY telegram from Milstein. Hoping for good news about work, any work, I was pressure-cooked for more than an hour in the telephone cabin in Fuengirola's brown-stained post office before tenuous connection was made.

When, at last, I got through, Milstein said, 'How's it going? Can I come and stay for a bit?'

I said, 'Stay? Sure. How long for?'

'Few days. Maybe a week. All right if I bring someone?'

'Someone? Who?'

'Someone I met. She admires you.'

Her name was Lucy Lowenstein; she was 'in publicity'. She was blonde and bouncy and dark-eyed and she wore beige overalls and not a lot else. Her admiration turned out to be for a novel about north London Jews which she thought I had written, but in fact had not. If Milstein had brought some small gift, say a box of Maltesers, for the children, Sylvia and I might have welcomed him with greater sincerity. But he had packed in a hurry and could offer only a copy of the *New Statesman* in which Henry Cake's latest anti-war play had a three-column rave. Milstein was going to get him to write a film unless I finished ours pretty soon. I told him I had an idea to do a modern dress Don Quixote; he said to forget it, stick to Larry Pleasure.

Milstein's appetite was a challenge even to Salvadora, and certainly to our budget. 'Mind if I take a bit more?' was the prelude to his leaning across the table for whatever seemed good to him long before we had finished our first helpings. 'OK if I borrow the car while you're working?' was his regular morning question and an empty tank its regular afternoon condition.

He found the twin beds in the spare room a bit limiting, so he asked if we would mind letting him and Lucy have our big bed, because – being married – we obviously didn't need it. Neither he nor Lucy managed to play with, or address a single word to, our children during their entire stay. On their last morning, Milstein asked me to drive him and Lucy to Gibraltar, because the bus left at the wrong time for their flight. 'It'll also give you a chance to buy some butter that isn't as rancid as that stuff she's been putting on the table.'

During the Sixties, Milstein went from Lucy to Samantha, and from Samantha to Jilly, and from Jilly to Bernadette, from Bernadette to Wendy and, of course, from strength to strength in the entertainment business. Thanks to the sales of my Fuengirola novel, and the film offer that followed it, Sylvia and I were able to move from Spain to Rome, and from Rome to Greece. Milstein jetted in to Rome and spent a week that turned into eleven days in our flat with Jilly. While he huddled with Michelangelo and Monica, Jilly developed severe toothache which required a series of unexpectedly expensive visits to our dentist. Milstein promised that she would pay us when we returned to London, but he was with Bernadette by then, and could hardly be responsible for Jilly's debts. He could give me her number if I really wanted.

After a long season in Rome, we went to Greece. We had the luck to buy a very simple house on a wide scimitar of then unspoiled Cycladic beach. Our children were now only just young enough not to need routine schooling; we lived in idyllic seclusion, conscious that its lease was brief. One very hot day, when we were having a siesta, Sylvia woke to hear a strange slapping noise on the flag-stoned terrace. I went, with aggressive apprehension, to see what it was.

The intruder was wearing a snorkelling mask and flippers and spear-fishing equipment was slung over a shoulder still beaded with drops of the Aegean.

'Hi,' Milstein said. 'Got anything to drink?'

I said, 'How the hell did you get here?'

'You still haven't got the telephone. Why?'

'I don't want the telephone,' I said.

'Yes, you do.' He was pointing to the two-masted yacht which was at anchor in our bay. 'Came on that.'

'How's Bernadette?'

'Wendy,' he said. 'She's fine. We've got Henry on the boat with us; he's with Jilly now. It's Sidney and Jackie's. He's putting money into the Don.'

'Henry? The Don?'

'Cake. He's scripting my new picture. *The Don*. I had this idea to do a modern dress Don Quixote. Anywhere decent to eat around here?'

'We're on a Greek island,' I said. 'There's a taverna which isn't bad and that's it.'

'How about that beer?' he said.

That evening, we took them up to Kosta's in the village. Our children came with us, of course, but everyone was too busy, and Henry Cake was too drunk, to say anything to them. Since I was the only person with any Greek, I did the ordering and, in due course, I called for the bill, which – although no great command of Greek was required to pay it – was also left to me. We were not sorry when the *Argo* sailed early the next morning, but – since we were living in London by that time – it would not have hurt Henry or Sidney or Milstein himself to ask us to the première of *The Don*.

During the Seventies, Sylvia and I found a house in the Dordogne, where we are able to spend our time immune from stress or envy. When quite recently rather precise rumours reached us that the Milstein Company was facing imminent financial rescheduling, I tried to feel dismayed, but my slow rift with Milstein was now deep enough for his misfortunes not to keep me awake at night. My shameful lack of true sympathy drove me to telephone his office. He certainly sounded very low. Somehow I gathered the impression that the bailiffs were removing the furniture as we spoke. Playing the old friend, I reminded him that London was not the world. 'The weather down here is magnificent,' I heard myself saying, 'you should get away from it all.'

There was a pause. 'Look,' he said, 'if I come, can I bring someone?'

'You mean Wendy?'

'Harriet.'

They stayed and they stayed. Sylvia cooked meals which, for all the thanks she received, might have fallen like manna from a bountiful sky. We took them to our favourite restaurants, where Milstein soon began to snap his fingers for restorative second bottles. Though his appetite improved, and neither he nor Harriet ever saw anything they liked on the *prix-fixe* menu, I understood, of course, that he was far too broke to pay his share. To add to the gloom, Harriet showed understandable signs of being bored with Milstein's moods.

They went back to London on the Monday and on the Wednesday my agent called to ask if I had heard the news. The Milstein Company had been bought up by a New York corporate raider for eighteen million pounds. Not long ago, I heard that Milstein had bought a château in the Aveyron, only a two-hour drive from us. When he telephoned, I must confess that I was gratified.

'Look,' he said, 'you must come over and see this place, obviously, because it's so much, much more beautiful than yours.'

'We should be delighted,' I said.

'Only right now we've got gardeners, we've got decorators . . .'

'We can wait,' I said. 'Harriet must be very happy.'

'Marie-Thérèse,' he said. 'I'm with Marie-Thérèse now. Look, this place honestly isn't habitable. Can I bring her over, just for a bit?'

They arrive tomorrow.

Waiting for
Marilyn

Janice Galloway

Janice Galloway is the award-winning author of THE TRICK IS TO KEEP BREATHING and BLOOD. Her latest novel is FOREIGN PARTS. She lives in Glasgow.

WAITING FOR MARILYN was first broadcast on Radio 3.

Waiting for Marilyn

ƨɒnoM

ƨɒnoM

Mona's flashes backwards behind the net.

Multicoloured plastic strips shield a cavity in the wall that isn't a door. They drift aside every so often, gusting like plant fronds while you peer into the black hole beneath. Nothing happens but you keep sitting, your hair in wet rags, listening to what pass for love songs on some terrible local station through the chalk-scrape of interference. Brittle as hell. Waiting for Marilyn.

You never asked for her. Didn't, now you think, even know what her name was till the third appointment but that's whose you are. The receptionist says so: a child-woman with black-rimmed eyes and the fringe like rotten teeth, a breast or a target shaved into the stubble on her head and a smile like a meat slice. Marilyn's, aren't you? When she said it this time, the purple stuff on her lips creased. She smiles that way even when you don't look. Especially when you don't look. It means she knows. Even if you don't she does. You're definitely Marilyn's.

Walk this way.

You follow holding the loose ties of the pinny they gave you, not able to remember from last time how it's meant to do up, hoping nobody's looking. Only one free basin. Tomato-soup red and white checks appear in the mirror as you hove into view, your hands the wrong way round tying a double knot. Trying not to feel like someone's grandma, a trattoria table; you sit, take the towel when it's offered, wait as you're told. When you lower your neck down to where the sink might be, the muscles in your belly take the strain, levelling you backwards gently. And still the cold enamel comes up too fast, biting the warmth under the hairline. It sucks like a catfish, your skin tensing fast enough to hurt but the other feeling does not abate. A low excitement in the belly, something that might be called butterflies. The same feeling. Through the mid-Atlantic Glasgow DJ roaring for Sonja's seventeenth CONGRATS AND MIND HOW YOU GO OUT THERE SONJA, through the start of a tune that files your fillings, even when the shower touches first time. Through the repeated strokes of cool water you can still feel it fluttering, swallowing like a fish. The sensation of waiting. Waiting for Marilyn.

Nothing past the fringing.

The junior goes through shouting for Rita. You don't know the junior's name but she washed your hair, wrapped it wet inside the towel, twisting it too tight. You would have said but she wasn't looking. She didn't speak either, just walked you across the floor holding your arm like you were frail or fragile, taking tiny, footbound steps to the middle chair. The seat was burst, stitches big as bite marks over the open red gash: a trail of wet dots tagged your heels like a stray. You settled yourself over the healing plastic scar and waited some more. You wait still, watching the doorless hole gape and close, appear and fold itself away again behind the tease of strips. They nudge a little in the heat haze from dryers while you wait, seeping, feeling the towel threaten to lose its anchor and fall to the floor. But you take a risk anyway, peer round.

On the left, the slatted muzzles of strung-up dryers grunt soundlessly behind two copper-coloured cans of spray. Net on a wire rope hides the misted window. On the right, six women ranged along the wallpaper stripes, frying. Under their electric drying hoods, wisps of silver and lilac stray down, making their faces pucker. Their hands turn pages, making dry sounds, louder than the radio. Half-price day for over-sixties. She said that the first time: We don't get many youngsters on a Wednesday, easing a scarlet comb down the back of your neck: I'm lucky to get you. Drawing the wet strands past your shoulders, checking its balance, her hands tucking under the sleek sheets. Then someone behind caught your eye, watching, and you turned away, waiting for the scissors, her tug on separate tresses. You recall the thud of a curl on your wrist, its slithering coolness. Your breath drawing in.

ꙅɒnoM

The sign flashes on and off backwards from this side of the glass.

Same chip on the formica ledge.

Scarlet clamps, coils of cable snaking along the hairy floor, slit-faced socket boards in the skirting, avoid the red blur in the mirror. But the plastic strips do not part. A movement in the corner of an eye is just the junior, hauling one of the row out from under her smoked perspex. We're ready to take your rods out, Mrs Dixon. Mrs Dixon smiles and is easily led. The three women left behind don't even notice. One is asleep: the last merely holds a magazine, staring. She can't close her eyes because the curlers under the hood stretch her skin too tight. Water makes a sheen over her eyes, a runnel to the cotton wool at the rim of the scarf. You turn away. The reflection of the junior slips past with a mug of coffee. The phone rings but no one goes. Mrs Dixon says thank you three times through repeated, unanswered ringing and your knuckles are white. Breathing deep and slow, deep and slow you try to keep your eyes from the unavoidable mirror. This is the DJ's favourite, he says, howling like a bitch in a shut room, his red-hot tip for the top. Diffuser discs with their rubber teats on the ledge in front, a lavender-tinted magazine you do not want to read. You shut your eyes, and lower your shoulders. You are almost relaxed when it happens.

Something clicks.
Metal against metal.

You raise your eyes and Marilyn is there in the mirror, mouthing hello. Your skull tilting in her hands and Marilyn looking in the glass, checking you over with her fingertips.

Right we are, she says, lifting a comb from nowhere you can see. The usual? Marilyn lowering the scarlet teeth. Just tidy you up a wee bit, then?

A tug sears then relaxes, burning at the roots.

Yes, you say, just the same.

And she smiles and concentrates, the tip of her tongue

appearing as she combs out your hair, wondering how much she'll take off.

That much OK?

The burr in the voice when she settles her hand on your shoulder to promise no more than an inch, you'll hardly notice. Her breath smells of milk. No more than an inch.

She steps back to begin. For the first time, you notice her clothes. Shorts and a loose shirt. Khaki. She wears things you wouldn't dare. Not knowing what to do with your hands, you watch her, Marilyn in army colours, raking her fingertips through the dead and drowned extremes of your being. It is you she handles with such seriousness, something you made from within your own body, opening the scissors carefully, bearing down and smiling to let you know it's OK. It's OK. Her familiar whisper. Then something new. Something small glitters at the roots of her fingers. One finger. She sees you looking, embarrassed and pleased before you drop your gaze.

Engagement ring, she says. Wee diamond.

The material of her shorts crushes against your arm.

I like solitaires.

A shear and flutter.

Marilyn is cutting your hair.

Marilyn with her slim hand cuffed to some absent man.

Despite you, your spine flinches, your throat constricts. Not able not to think. Slicing metal. A man in this choking female interior. You imagine greased-back hair and a square jaw, jeans and a pristine teeshirt, a thin-lipped mouth swallowing hers. His mouth leaves marks: tiny weals on a small white breast. Marilyn's arm changes colour as the sign flashes. Half her face turns pale blue. You glance at the old women, back again, not wanting to see any more. The back of his hand wrapping a stretched-tight bolt of red flesh, nuzzling it against her leg. The cushion he would make of her. You crush your eyes tight, hoping so loud you almost speak. I hope he's not heavy.

Sorry?

Marilyn's slip of a girlness wondering what it was you said. Is everything OK? And you say fine, laughing to make it truer: Just talking to myself. And she smiles and resumes. Her pale mouth. Looking down to hide your blush and seeing her shorts wide of her skin, the way the cloth lifts to make a tunnel at her thigh. Wide enough for a hand to slip inside.

The finger glitters as she tilts your head forward. A split-second of your own face, expressionless, appears as you go down, shutting its eyes again to wait for her touch on the nape of your neck.

The smug bastard on the radio keeps going.

sɐnoM flashes backwards from the other side of the glass.

Some Metal Buildings

Buildings

Geoff Nicholson

Geoff Nicholson is the author of eight novels. Most recent are THE FOOD CHAIN, THE ERROL FLYNN NOVEL and EVERYTHING AND MORE. At the moment he is writing a novel about fetishism provisionally called *Footsucker*. He lives in London.

SOME METAL BUILDINGS was broadcast on Radio 4 and read by Imelda Staunton.

∫

Some Metal Buildings

ONE

Ralph and Irena were looking for affordable luxury and they liked to think they'd found it. They lived in a flexible-plan single-storey house built around a small, decorative courtyard. And even though they hadn't been blessed with children, they were happy.

Ralph, moving with surprising grace for a large man, gathered up the post as it spilled through the letter box and took it into the kitchen where his wife Irena was weaving her breakfast culinary magic.

'Letter for you,' he said casually. 'Looks like junk.'

But he was wrong. It was a catalogue for maintenance-free, steel garden sheds with zinc coating and baked-on coloured finish.

Irena tore open the envelope and riffled through the pages of the catalogue. She observed the solid construction and careful engineering of the sheds. She read that they were easy to erect and came flat-packed for convenience.

She admired the way they were designed to harmonise with almost any environment.

Ralph saw what his wife was reading, and asked, 'Do we need a steel shed in our lives?'

'Everyone needs a steel shed in their lives,' said Irena, noticing that the French toast was about to burn.

TWO

Next day Irena should have been at work but instead she went to the Museum of Mankind to see an exhibition called 'Paradise: Change and Continuity in the New Guinea Highlands'.

It was a show about the life of the Wahgi, a race that had never encountered outsiders until about sixty years ago. It showed their customs, their ceremonies, their crafts; but most of this was of only passing interest to Irena. What really grabbed her attention was the exhibition's replica of a Wahgi 'trade-store'.

This was a chunky, sturdy structure, about the size of a single garage. It resembled an old-fashioned newspaper kiosk, with a sloping roof and a door and an open counter in the front. On the wall was a sign that said, 'No ken askim long dinan', which translates as 'Don't ask for credit'. Irena wouldn't dream of it.

Inside the trade-store, displayed on shelves, were scarfs, shirts, toys, balls of wool, and tins of meat loaf, dripping and 'banana-flavoured roll'.

Irena looked and learned. There's at least one of these trade-stores per Wahgi community and, as well as selling goods, they're used as places to store 'men's love magic', which injures the health of women and children if kept at home.

Irena found all this interesting enough but it still wasn't

what really fascinated her. What really fired her imagination was the fact this store was made out of unpainted corrugated iron. How come? Because, an explanatory label said, if someone tries to break into the store it makes a helluva lot of noise.

Irena smiled blissfully to herself and wondered to what extent the use of corrugated iron in architecture is a touchstone of human civilisation.

THREE

A day or two later they were enjoying an extremely quaffable bottle of Don Zolio luxury sherry and Irena said to Ralph, 'Corrugated iron was invented in the late 1820s and was to revolutionise building techniques. From the late 1830s prefabricated buildings made of corrugated iron were being shipped from this country to all parts of the globe; to California and Australia, to Africa and India; all kinds of buildings; bungalows, shooting lodges, hospitals, chapels, churches.'

'I see,' said Ralph savouring the deep velvety fino. 'And I suppose you want to spend the rest of your life going round the world looking at them.'

'At last,' thought Irena, 'a man, who understands.'

But she thought wrong.

FOUR

Ralph didn't mind too much when, later that same year, they went away for a long weekend to the Peak District, and visited the village of Youlgreave. It was the wrong season for well-dressing, nevertheless they found much to admire: the air, the limestone hills, the river, the old Co-op now converted into a Youth Hostel. But Irena was there for quite other reasons.

At the top of a lane that led down into the valley, she stopped to admire the scout hut, a two-storey building made of green corrugated iron. It had a black corrugated roof, smart red curtains at the windows, and a simple but effective portico, also made of corrugated iron.

'Gosh,' she said, not entirely to herself.

She stood in quiet admiration. It was a good half hour before poor Ralph could persuade her to come to the tea room with him.

FIVE

She discovered a metal church in Kilburn, next to the RSPCA, now used as a headquarters by some sort of youth project.

It had Gothic doorways and lancet windows, a tower, and the base to which a spire might be attached. It was painted in two shades of institutional blue, and across one metal wall someone, perhaps a well-wisher, had sprayed the slogan 'Toys not Guns'. In Kilburn this felt like progress.

SIX

Irena thought of Mary Kingsley. Wasn't it she who, in *Travels in West Africa*, wrote:

> Corrugated iron is my abomination. I do not attack it from an aesthetic viewpoint (just as well, thinks Irena). There is, close to Christianborg Castle, at Acara, Gold Coast, a patch of bungalows and offices . . . that . . . in the hard,

bright sunshine look like an encampment of snow white tents among the cocoa palms. But the heat inside . . .

Irena had never given much thought to the thermal properties of corrugated iron, but she now realised this was good advice and resolved never to live in a metal building in West Africa.

SEVEN

That night she and Ralph made love. He nuzzled his head against her ample breasts and said, 'What is it with you and metal buildings?'

She stroked his dense biceps and said girlishly, 'I think it's about morality or rather its absence. One hears so much about architecture as a force for social good, as something holy with an agenda and a philosophy. But a metal building has none of that. It has no architect, no pretension. It is morally blank.'

'Now hold your horses,' Ralph said as he drew her close to him. 'You yourself have described metal churches to me.'

'Yes, and they're morally blank too,' she said, her body crackling with coiled, sexual energy.

'A morally blank church,' he said with a gush. 'Now I've heard everything.'

But he hadn't.

EIGHT

Irena's work attendance record got worse and worse. Sometimes she took days from her holiday entitlement, but more often she simply called in sick. She spent a lot of time following her special interest.

She visited allotments to look at more sheds. She went in search of lock-up garages, lean-tos, Nissen huts, aircraft hangars, barns, warehouses, factories.

She visited a number of gas holders and she went to Paris in order to climb the Eiffel Tower, though she realised there were those who would argue that both gas holders and towers were structures rather than buildings.

She got particularly excited about a polyhedral metal construction adjacent to the Newport Pagnell Services on the M1 which was used to store road salt.

Ralph, who liked to think of himself as an understanding man, increasingly failed to understand.

NINE

She swung it so that she could get to go to a conference in California. Once there she skived off the lectures and seminars and went out in her rented car admiring car washes, body shops, the colourful metal shacks of dispossessed indigenous peoples. She picked up a cute hitchhiker and took him back to her room at the Motel 6.

When she got home she told Ralph it had been the trip of a lifetime.

TEN

And then one day, for no reason she could think of, she got in her Ford Mondeo, found herself driving up the A12, and before long was in Saxmundham. She looked for a place to stop, found the car park behind the Gateway supermarket, and as she brought her car to a halt, a wonderful sight loomed up in front of her.

She saw a large imposing metal building, two storeys

high, some sixty feet by forty, probably agricultural in origin, painted burnt ochre, and most importantly of all, with an estate agent's board attached to the side. The building was to let.

A few swift negotiations and the building was hers. She took possession. She moved in. Then she bought a small Yamaha electronic keyboard and installed it in a corner of her building. At various times of the day or night, though never at offensive volume, Irena could be heard playing standards on her new instrument, old favourites such as 'Autumn Leaves', 'These Foolish Things', 'In the Wee Small Hours of the Morning', and 'The Night We Called It A Day', to name only four.

ELEVEN

A distressed Ralph, wanting Irena more than ever in her absence, came to visit.

'Does our love count for nothing?' he asked.

'Consider this,' Irena replied. 'You are married to a woman who only has eyes for metal buildings. Ask yourself, "Is there iron in my soul?" If the answer is no, you can draw your own conclusions.'

'Poor Irena,' he thought. 'This will not bring her happiness and the love of a good man.'

But he was wrong again.

TWELVE

Then, early one June morning, she heard the snivel of an approaching diesel engine. She threw back one of the sliding metal doors and saw that a lightweight Land Rover had pulled up outside her building. A man got out, a real man. He was tough, wiry, suntanned, hirsute, part poet, part adventurer. His face was supremely strong and rugged, though not insensitive.

'Allow me to introduce myself,' he said. 'The name's Dan. Just plain Dan. I'm an engineer. I specialise in building multi-million gallon tanks and towers for rural water developments, mostly in South America. And I'd just like to say, that's some metal building you've got there.'

'Ah,' she said, 'my knight in shining armour.'

Summer Houses

Philip Hensher

Philip Hensher was born in London and educated in Yorkshire, Oxford and Cambridge. He has reviewed for the *Guardian*, *The Spectator* and the *Daily Telegraph*. His first novel, OTHER LULUS was published in 1994, his second KITCHEN VENOM will be published later this year. He is collaborating on an opera, POWDER HER FACE to be premièred in July 1995 by Thomas Adés. He lives in South London.

SUMMER HOUSES was read by Sylvestra Le Touzel and broadcast on Radio 4.

S

Summer Houses

When my father returned from America, I hardly knew him and he was a capitalist. My grandmother pushed me forward in the dark hallway of her flat in Přisker street. I went towards a man I could hardly see.

'Look,' she said. 'It's your daughter.'

He stretched out his hand, a strange gesture to offer a ten-year-old girl, but I took it and we shook. I had been trussed up in party wear by my grandmother, and the elastic and ribbons cutting into my skin made me accept formality.

'What a man,' my grandmother said, turning and going back into the kitchen. My father looked at me gravely.

My brother was too small to remember anything about my father, and refused to touch him or to look at anything – except the back of the chair he was hiding behind.

'Is that Bedřich?' my father said. I nodded. 'A baboon.' I nodded. 'And why is he sniffing?'

I didn't say anything. Bedřich's nose was usually running.

'Does he know who I am?'

'I've told him all about you.' This was true.

'What have you told him?' I hung my head and looked at my feet. 'Do you remember me?'

'Bits,' I said. My brother used to ask me if I remembered our father, and I would say yes.

'Tell me,' he would say.

'He's very tall, and he lives in America.'

'How did he get to America?'

'He flew.' We accepted that, then.

'Is he coming back?'

'He promised me he would.'

'When?' Bedřich would say.

'Soon.' I knew nothing about it.

'What's he going to bring us?'

'Oh, chocolate and chewing gum, and an American car, a big one.' I saw these bright parcels, and Bedřich accepted them.

Anyway, Bedřich was crouched behind the chair and not looking at anything. He was wiping his nose on the sleeve of his sweater. My father poked at him with the sole of his foot. Bedřich said something. I got down beside him.

'It's father,' I said.

'Has he got any presents for us?'

'What did he say?' said my father.

'He asked if you had brought any presents back from America for him.'

'What a baboon,' said father.

He didn't have a car from America, at least not then, and we went back to the flat we had all been born in by taxi. Bedřich looked at him with his mouth open. He ignored Bedřich, and talked to me.

'How old are you now?'

'Ten.'

'Do you go to school?'

'Yes.'

'Of course. Do you like it?'

'Bits.'

'What do you like best?'

'Geography.'

'How much will you give me for fifty American dollars,' he said then to the taxi-driver.

The driver didn't respond, and Father said it again.

The taxi-driver looked at him warily in the mirror.

'What fifty American dollars.'

'Some of the American dollars I've got in my pocket.'

There was a silence. The taxi-driver named an enormous sum. Bedřich, thinking he was going to get his present, began to tug at father's arm. 'Papa.'

'Ha,' said father. He didn't get his fifty American dollars out, and sank back in the seat.

'Shitface,' said the driver.

'Just curiosity,' said Father.

I hung back a little from the unfamiliar flat as father unlocked the door.

'It's all right,' said Father. 'There's no one there.'

'Are we going to live here now?' I asked.

'For a while.'

The flat seemed lived in. We went in slowly and looked around us as if it was in a foreign country.

'Can you cook?' said Father, and it hardly occurred to me that he could be talking to me. I had never cooked in my life.

'No.'

'It doesn't matter. We won't be staying very long.'

Father did no work. And if he went out he left after we had gone to school and came back before. There were no presents, and after a few days Bedřich had taken Father into his promising but already disappointed world without comment. Father had no idea of housekeeping, and when food came, it came in large amounts, without warning. And it was crated. If Father had a friend who was selling oddly coloured American drinks in boxes of forty-eight, or strange tinned beans, then that would be it. Occasionally Father would come home with an unplucked chicken that someone had offered him, or half a pig. We did well enough out of Father's strokes of luck and dealings, but our meals, though festive, were unlike normal meals.

My father used to say that things would soon change. And one day he called me into the drawing room and asked me if I liked living with grandmother in Pařisker street. I nodded.

'Did you prefer it to this?'

'No.'

'Good girl. But I think you're going to have to live with her again.'

'Are we all going to live with her?'

'Just you and Bedřich.'

'Are you going to America again?'

'No. I'm going to be in Prague still.'

'Where will you live?'

'I'm going to live in the summer house.' I took a while to think about this.

'Why can't we all live here?'

'Because somebody else is going to.'

'Who?'

'Americans.'

Because we lived in the centre of Prague, and because there was no garden near us, we had a plot of land in the suburbs where we grew flowers. All the time father had been in America my grandmother and I had looked after it. On each plot there was a green-painted hut, where you sat and looked at your garden. There was a wooden cool-box in ours, where you could put your lunch. I had long before been allowed to paint the box, in stripes, which my grandmother had shown me how to keep even with bits of tape. There was a bed which I would nap on when I was small, in the afternoons, and two wooden chairs, one of which had broken and was never used.

Every gardener, I suppose, had a different word for their green hut. We called ours 'the summer house', because we only used it in the summer. It was this that Father was going to go and live in.

'Which Americans?'

'I don't know which Americans. But lots of Americans come to Prague, you know. They've got to stay somewhere.'

'Don't they stay in hotels?'

'Not when they see our flat.'

When this was explained to my grandmother, she was indignant. But not as much as when father moved us in and left straight away. I asked her why father was living in the summer house.

'Because he wants to make money.'

'How?'

'It doesn't cost him anything to live in the summer house, and these rich Americans who want to live in Prague are going to pay him money to live in the flat.'

'How much are they going to pay?'

'I don't want to know,' said my grandmother. It seemed quite sensible to me, but she was almost speechless.

Father moved out and we moved out. No one seemed to be moving in. My grandmother kept telling us of the progress of the flat. 'He can't rent it out to anyone,' she said.

'You'll have to redecorate it, it's far too shabby for Americans.' He did. 'It's the wrong time of the year, who comes to Prague now? You might as well move back in.' My father wouldn't, and we all carried on living separately.

Father spent the summer eating cold food in the summer house and waiting for the rich Americans to turn up. We only saw him when he came round to Grandmother's for something hot and to listen to her complaints. She always said that he wasn't fair to her, and she wasn't putting up with it. And when we were old enough we wouldn't put up with it either. We just watched him eating enough for three, until Grandmother had to tell us to eat as well.

Bedřich was so young I don't think he really understood what was going on, or perhaps he just didn't believe it. The strange thing was that before long his favourite people were the Americans who never turned up. He invented a whole family of Americans who were living in our flat, living exciting lives. Usually after lunch he would say, 'Let's go and see the Americans.' I humoured him, because I wanted to believe in the Americans too.

'Who do you like best, Grandmother or Father or the Americans?'

'I like the Americans best.'

'Or do you like bacon best?' I said, teasing him.

'No. I like the Americans best.' Then he'd sniffle, and I'd tell him to stop it.

There were three of them, a girl and two boys, in Bedřich's mind. One boy was called Tony, and the girl was called Catherine and the third one was called Dud.

'Dud?'

'Yes. He's the nicest.'

I went along with it. 'Let's go and see Tony and Catherine and Dud.'

'No,' Bedřich said.

'Let's go and see Father, then,'

'No.'

I told Father, and he laughed. Then he asked if I'd learnt any English from talking to them, these Americans. I said the English words that I could remember, all in a line, and a few that we'd made up, and then he laughed again.

'Good girl. I think we'll be moving back fairly soon.'

That winter seemed more boring than ever, when even Bedřich had decided the Americans had gone. We didn't move back into the flat. Father tried to keep on living in the summerhouse, since he'd finally managed to let the flat: to a Russian colonel and his family. They paid hardly any money, and after the first two months they stopped paying at all. But in a way it was a matter of pride that Father had found a tenant for the flat, and I don't think he minded at first. For almost a month more he lived in the summerhouse in the cold, with just an electric fire, running off a car battery. And then one day, two panes of glass shattered in the frost, and he had to admit defeat. He finally agreed with my grandmother that the summer house was impossible. He tried to evict the Russian colonel from the flat, but when that proved impossible, as everyone told him, he moved to my grandmother's where we all were now.

Sometimes when the snow melts everything seems to change. But when spring came, nothing was different. We carried on living with my grandmother, and we carried on fighting and arguing. My father never really got any more polite to Bedřich, though I see it must have been annoying when spring came and Bedřich's cold didn't get any better. That year it just seemed to get worse. We made the same jokes about it as ever, which my father didn't join in with. I suppose it was the joking which stopped us from taking Bedřich seriously. So it was my father who actually noticed that it was getting towards the end of May and Bedřich was not just sniffing, but coughing, quite heavily. And shivering.

When Bedřich died, I sat down to write letters. But I

didn't have anyone to write to, really. Anyone who would have cared knew. So I found myself writing a long letter to Tony and Catherine and Dud. Those funny healthy people. I told them all about it, a long letter. I wish I could say I did it because Bedřich had asked me to in the hospital. But I didn't. I addressed it to Tony and Catherine and Dud, America, and I posted it. For a while I even looked at the letters that arrived, in case something, somehow, came back.

As for Father, well, when we moved back into the flat after the Russian colonel finally left of his own free will, he decided that he wouldn't move out again, or rent it to foreigners. And he started buying odd crates of food just like he had before, and making his money in ways no one really wanted to understand. And he still does. We live close to each other now. I love my father, but I don't see much of him any more.

To Her Unready Boyfriend

Helen Simpson

Helen Simpson's first collection of short stories, FOUR BARE LEGS IN A BED, won the *Sunday Times* Young Writer of the Year and the Somerset Maugham awards. Her suspense novella, FLESH AND GRASS, appeared with Ruth Rendell's THE STRAWBERRY TREE under the general title UNGUARDED HOURS. In 1993 she was chosen as one of *Granta*'s twenty Best Young British Novelists. She has just finished a play, PINSTRIPE. Her second volume of stories will be published this year.

TO HER UNREADY BOYFRIEND was read by Jane Whittenshaw, and broadcast on Radio 4.

∫

To Her Unready Boyfriend

If time sprawled ahead of us in a limitless and improving vista, your reluctance to consider the future wouldn't matter a scrap. We could lie in bed all afternoon browsing through the atlas to map out our itinerary for the next couple of decades or so.

We would discuss the politics of regions shaded in fondant pink and yellow and pistachio, skip to and fro across the equator, splash through the Tasman and Caspian seas, try our tongues round Kandy, Changchun, La Paz, Minsk. I would see you, racoon-furred and seal-booted in the winds of Nova Scotia, paddling our canoe from Natashquan to Sept-Iles, where we would disembark and joyfully climb up to and across the Otish mountains. At the ancient stadium of Olympia, to the susurrous applause of silver leaves we would take our marks on the line where Greek athletes crouched two thousand years ago, then race each other across a hundred yards, repeatedly. Our love would keep us young, along with the judicious use of facial oils, rowing machines, avoidance of strong sunlight, and capsules of Royal Jelly. We would keep our options open.

Your fondness for dubiety, the way you prize the fluid and infinite possibilities which unfurl before an unattached person, these I sympathise with utterly. You cry freedom and I hear you. Harbouring the sense that there's an epiphany just around the corner, you wait, breath bated, creatively passive, for the chance phrase or glance that will crystallise it all, show you what your life is about and where it is leading. You lack the desire to commit yourself. You tell me you are not ready for the responsibility of a child, and why should you be, my darling? You're only thirty-six.

We have loved each other for over ten years now, but the night we met for the first time is like a photograph I carry in my wallet, clear as clear. I sat there in the White Hart, one of a group round a crowded table in a cloud of smoke. We hadn't spoken, you hadn't even seen me, but I was smitten by your heroic frowning profile, the stream of talk (of which I remember not one word, but it was in some way didactic, exhortatory), the glowing cigarette and your excitable hands transferring it to and from your mouth between castles of rhetoric. I wasn't particularly interested in what you were saying, but I wanted to be near you in the way I want to be near a successful log fire. I felt this so strongly I was afraid it would show, so I kept my eyes down, strictly away from your glamorous felty greatcoat, I adjusted my movement as my body swivelled towards you, heliotropic, like a plant towards the sun.

You got up and went to the bar for a round of drinks. Everyone else carried on talking, took no notice. To me it was as if a tooth had been pulled. By your place at the table was an overflowing ashtray and the box of matches you'd been using. I don't smoke. I leaned over, oh so casually, and hooked up that box of matches. I hid it in my hand, a gentle fist around it. Later I examined my trophy in private, sniffed the gunpowder smell and pushed out the miniature drawer with my thumb. Then I struck one of the precious batons and let the flame burn down until it reached my fingers. Ouch.

Since then you have rowed your boat less than merrily with increasing lassitude down the stream of time to the point where you now give it so little direction that you are in fact all but drifting. As long as outside events, not personal choice, make things happen, you can accept change with a good enough grace. Staying passive, you reason, is as though you haven't made a choice and your central purity is untouched.

Another woman might start to think of engineering an accident.

But imagine, just imagine if time were to dawdle and lose itself, as I wish it would; if the laws of mutability were to go a little bit haywire in our case; then perhaps one tender blue-grey evening in the third millennium we might find ourselves sitting by the fireside in our late fifties, our eyes would meet, and we would know we were ready at last. Our mortgage would be negligible by then, your thesis would at last be lapped in gold-tooled leather, and the worst of our wanderlust would be slaked. Hand in hand we would climb the stairs that night to start a baby. And not before.

For, my dear love, you deserve acres of time, long red carpets of it; nor would I wish any less for you.

But, my sweet eternal boy, in recent months I've been dogged by a rhythmic noise, soft but distinct, tick-*tock*, tick-*tock* like the crocodile in Peter Pan. I've reached a certain age, you must remember, and this wretched clock noise, which increases in volume as the day progresses and is at its most distracting, menacing even, just when I'm undressing for bed, warns me, *Get*-a-move-on *hur*ry-up, *Get*-a-move-on *not*-much-time.

It's all right for you, you're like the popes in the Renaissance, you can go on fathering children till you're eighty-three. But if you want us to stay together, and I say this as one who as you know has never used emotional blackmail in all our years together, if you want us to stay together, I say, then you must start telling the time by my clock. I can't ignore it.

You may prefer, of course, to wait another ten or fifteen years, as in my fireside fantasy. You may prefer to wait for the arrival of a paunch and root canal work before at last sowing the long-hoarded seed. If so, I won't be there. I'll be somewhere else, giggling with my adolescent daughter.

You say, our love for each other is enough, my talk is dangerously hubristic, let's take each day as it comes.

The trouble with that is, whether we like it or not we can't stay the same. It's not allowed. There's no procedure for freezing our present happiness, no insurance scheme against future grief or coldness or misunderstanding. Love fails. Desire fades. Like rags of crumpled linen we'll be out in the cold wind, whirling.

We can't mark time ad infinitum. Meanwhile, to our dismay, this baby denial will start to appear increasingly as a match that's not been struck. The irony is that you're the one who goes on about death all the time. What's it all about? Is there just nothing at the end? Can't you see this is your one sure way of cocking a snook at all that? All right, eventually, I admit, you will be forced by the laws of physics to unlink your molecules, to crumble into motes and spores and polycarbons, and your strongest comfort is that you might with luck become part of the atmosphere. But if your child is at the bedside when you draw your last breath, a child with your hunted look, your heroic profile, new-minted, then the baton will have been passed on.

Forgive me, too, for pointing this out, my love, but there is something lugubrious and loose-endish about you, a central glumness that my charming presence hasn't managed to melt entirely. I see the way you drink, your lack of joie de vivre. You can warm your hands at the fire of other people's high jinks, but in your own kitchen there is a sadness, as of an uncooked cake.

You're unfinished, some sort of refugee, abandoned early on and – despite my best efforts – not yet rescued.

The longer you live like this, solipsistic, infinitely retractable, the more unkind life will appear, and you will increasingly feel capable of less and less.

A child would alter the balance between us, a child would turn the direction of our eyes away from the withering and fattening of our overfamiliar selves towards the pleasure of a fresh new presence growing.

You're wonderfully perspicacious, irresistibly beautiful, and you say I've pulled you out of the miseries that used to plague you. I can however only do so much for you; some mothering of course; but I am *not* your mother.

I would *like* to be a mother, not yours but still a mother. For this, though, I want your consent.

See me through nine months. I want to be a nice ripe pear on the sunwarmed bricks of a walled garden.

He'd look just like you. He could curl up in the crook of your arm at night. He'd stare at you in amazement at first, with a dazzled china-blue frown. When he meowed you could pass him over to me, I'd calm him down. I'd do it all, you wouldn't even notice.

Or perhaps we might have a girl, a baby girl, and after hacking through all those tiresome thorn-hedged years you would at last have found your own princess. You are capable of such generous secret tenderness that I think you couldn't fail to be a father both adoring and adored.

Let me see if I can draw a parallel to make you understand. I find it very peculiar that someone so clever can be so obtuse.

Do you remember the last time we saw Celia, just after she'd moved to the little house in Ansty with its south-facing garden, do you remember how she said she was home at last, this was the place she wanted to live in for the rest of her life? And as an acknowledgement of this fact she had planted a fig tree, knowing full well that she wouldn't be seeing any fruit on its branches for a good twenty-five years. I liked that. It was an act of faith. I'm fed up with us being so abjectly tentative.

If you carry on trying to rope us together with these massive cables of inertia, we'll fly apart at last. Time won't stand still just because we're lucky in love, more's the pity.

Now, then: let's move on now. Let's abandon our fastidious comforts, wave goodbye to our turtledove snuggery while there's still time. Come on. You can't keep yourself to yourself forever. Be brave! Let's jump before we're pushed.

Come to bed. Unprotected. Now.

Our Genius

Rober Cremins

Robert Cremins was born in Dublin in 1968. His short stories have been published in *Critical Quarterly, Paris Transcontinental* and *Passages*. Critical work has appeared in *The Irish Times*. He lives and teaches in Houston, Texas, where he is also working on his first novel.

OUR GENIUS was first broadcast on Radio 4, and read by Sean Campion.

∫

Our Genius

The view of Dublin from this room is panoramic, and on a very fine day like today, you can make out the Mourne Mountains in the North. My old room faces the bay, but that view was steadily spoilt by a neighbour's evergreens during my adolescence. When I was sixteen and Henry fifteen, I asked my parents if I could have this room. The answer was an instant no – it belonged to my brother.

I am writing at his worktable. It's as if he'd just stood up from it – around me are circuit-boards and chips, beakers and pipettes. But it's three years since he's been here. When it happened, I expected this detritus to be taken away, but nobody came, except the media.

One night when we were children – eight and nine – we stayed up late for our father's return from a business trip. He had, as always, a gift for us: a remote control tank.

'William,' he whispered, 'you know how your baby brother loves this kind of toy – let him go first.'

After muttering a protest, I agreed. My consent turned out to be irrelevant: the tank wouldn't work. My father slapped the control against his hand, tried the batteries of another appliance, read the instructions in both English and German – all in vain. We were packed off to bed with the weary promise that it would be examined tomorrow, the weekend.

I woke the next morning to a humming sound, and opened my eyes to see the tank crossing my rough carpet. In the doorway was Henry, remote control in his hands.

'How did you get it to work?'

He smiled and shrugged.

'I just kept on pressing the button.'

Our parents were delighted to see the tank rolling across the landing when they came out of their bedroom, and deeply amused when Henry told them how he'd repaired it. They went downstairs. My father, however, returned a few minutes later, frowning at what he was carrying in his hand – fragments of soft lead.

'These were on the kitchen floor, boys,' he said, looking up. 'Who was using my soldering-iron?'

He was astonished by his own question. There was silence; then Henry piped up: 'I was, Daddy.'

He received an immediate slap – not too hard – and several lectures in the days following the soldering. But I remember my parents' mood became gently festive: they'd realised one of their sons was a little genius. They fed the newly revealed creature books; he ate voraciously. I tried to become a more enthusiastic playmate, but he became less and less engaged by games. His new aloofness maddened me. I tried some basic bullying, but he endured the discomfort without comment, as if it were being caused by something as impersonal as a germ. As we headed into our teens, I tried to become a more intelligent friend instead, but he did no more than tolerate my conversation. He did however tell me his dreams, his bad dreams. One was about Belfast, a place we'd seen only on TV. He narrated it enthusiastically.

'It was nightfall and I was being chased by men in black

balaclavas. They caught me on waste ground and pinned me down. Their eyes were glowing through the slits in their masks. They took out butcher's knives, and then I woke up!'

It became my nightmare, too. I told him to keep his stupid dreams to himself. He did.

At the Jesuit school we attended, he excelled in mathematics, musical theory, and all disciplines of science. His own discipline, however, in the recurring words of school reports, left something to be desired. On one occasion he got a Saturday detention for pushing his lab partner's face an inch away from a flaming Bunsen burner. After that, he was made to work on his own; he didn't object.

My parents' reaction to this episode was to purchase the table I am writing at. They stated that whatever he was going to do here should be open to inspection, encouraging him to use the space for pleasant chemistry, elementary electronics – nice, safe work. Soon he was taking apart and rebuilding short-wave radios and primitive home computers. They would think about each of these experiments long and hard, and then give each of them their tentative blessing.

On the rare occasions that I was in and he was out, I would steal in here, lean over this table, and marvel at the evidence of my brother's twin skills: construction and deconstruction. I looked, but never touched a chip, fearing any tiny misplacement would give away my intrusion. I wouldn't be surprised if he was aware of this snooping; at the very least he had foreseen the risk, for some of his work was not on show.

I detected this hidden industry the autumn he turned fourteen. On Hallowe'en, neighbours of ours had a banger thrown through their letter box. Their five-year-old boy, who ran out from the kitchen when he heard the doorbell, wet himself; their carpet was scorched. Rough types seen in the neighbourhood that night were communally blamed. My father said he'd heard that bangers smuggled in from England were being hawked on Moore Street – why couldn't the gardai stop the sale of this miniature dynamite. I'd spent Hallowe'en in the local park with friends, setting off samples of the very product my father talked about. They'd been most disappointing, nothing like his advertisement. According to my parents, Henry had been in his room all evening. After visiting his desk a few days later, however, I discovered specks of black powder on my sweaty fingertips.

Henry did, surprisingly, develop one academic weakness: the Irish language. My parents were concerned: Irish was an entry requirement for the National University. Henry claimed he simply found the language difficult, even though he had no problem with his Latin and his French. My parents thought his progress was being frustrated because of a personality clash with his teacher, Mr O'hUiginn. It was true that Henry was constantly in trouble with the man. He would brag to me about these classes:

'Today, Higgins stopped talking Irish completely so everyone could understand his rant about how it's the duty of every Irishman to strive for the reintegration of the National Territory. But, of course, the goon slapped condemnation of violence on to the end of the lecture. That's when I asked him if he was a hypocrite, and that's when he threw me out of class.'

'Why do you have to be such a troublemaker?' I asked my brother.

He responded with a shrug.

His progress did not improve. After his next report card arrived, my father signed him up for two weeks in July at an Irish college. Henry told my parents he was not going:

'That *Gaeltacht* is closer to New York than Dublin.'

But when my father dangled a trip to a London science fair in front of him, Henry sourly assented to a fortnight in the West.

*   *   *

We were at Heuston Station to meet the train bringing him back. We stood behind the barrier, waving as soon as we saw him. He gave us no salute in return. And that was a black arm-band he was wearing. On our side of the barrier he put down his case, an inscrutable little smile on his lips. My parents looked at Henry as if they'd been sent back the wrong boy.

'Why on earth are you wearing that thing?' my father demanded.

'Didn't you hear, Dad?' said Henry, all surprise. 'A volunteer was killed in action.'

'Henry, *please* take it off.'

'*Ánraí is anim dom.*'

'Your name is *Henry*,' my father said.

'Henry is a West Brit name.'

'Henry is a *nice* name,' said my mother, emotional.

Other families were beginning to look at us.

'All right,' said my father. 'I'll call you Ánraí, if you take the armband off.'

Henry smiled again.

'Deal.'

The deal fell through. I refused to call him by his new name; my parents did so only when he corrected them, which he did constantly at first, then less as his London trip approached. By the time we were in the shadow of the new school year, it seemed his Gaelic phase was over. I braced myself for new trouble – but there was none. We became a studious pair. I finished school and started an arts degree. Henry chewed up the Leaving Certificate curriculum. He sat the big summer exams calmly. It was a given he would be swaddled in scholarship money when the results came out in late August. The Royal Dublin Society asked him to participate in their science summer school as a kind of prodigy-in-residence, and he agreed. My parents were happy people.

After passing my first year university exams, I went to

Strasbourg to work as a hotel receptionist. I received a letter from my parents all about Henry. He had backed out of the summer school, gone to London to stay with some people he knew from Irish college, and was working for a computer company. He would be back in time for the start of college. The letter didn't say whether or not they had objected to him going.

I worked the night shift. After midnight, with the lobby quiet, I would listen to the World Service. One night in early August, it reported a terrorist attack in London. My first reaction, soon smothered by logic, was that this latest bomb had exploded very close to home.

It had gone off beside the department store's display of Waterford Crystal. Two shoppers, one American, the other Irish, had been shredded to death by the wave of flying glass, two dozen others injured. The bomb had been set off, authorities believed, by a remote control device. The next night, I heard that an Irishman was being held under the Prevention of Terrorism Act. The following night, my father phoned me. He didn't talk, he telegraphed: 'Your brother is in trouble. We are on our way to London. Come home immediately.'

All I said was: 'I understand.'

I told my employers my brother was dead.

Travelling home, I felt some muddy substance moving slowly through my veins. It took me most of the journey to figure out what it was: shame. Shame for what he had done, and for what we had failed to do.

No organisation has ever claimed responsibility for the explosion; the usual suspects issued ambivalent denials at the time. There were several other detentions in connection with the case, never any arrests. The address that Henry had given my parents turned out to be a fiction. When he was detained – at a small hotel near Victoria Station – he had several stolen credit cards on him. It has never been proven that anybody gave him support the whole time he was in England. It seems appropriate – I cannot imagine Henry as part of a team.

Three years. Since Henry was not yet eighteen when he planted his bomb – how the quality papers over there marvelled at his sophistication – he is detained at Her Majesty's pleasure. A campaign has started, both here and across the water, to prove that they have got the wrong man. But I swear that this time they have got the right man. Indeed, Henry has never claimed to any of the politicians or priests who visit him that his confession – rich in technical detail – was beaten out of him or the result of a bad deal with the prosecution. My parents are fervently involved in the campaign. They are in England today, making their weekly prison pilgrimage. It is a costly habit: my father has sold his business, and this house is next. I am here today to sort some things out.

I have visited Henry just once. Through the thick glass, I asked him *why*. He responded with a shrug. I wished I could smash that window and get a proper answer out of him – for once. But that's how the meeting ended – with Henry's shrug.

But I will not let our story end like that. I want to conclude with a memory, one earlier than any of those I've described. We are in my father's study, my brother and I, looking up at a glazed map of the world, something my father inherited from his father. It is not like the world in our school atlas. So much of the Earth, including our own country, is coloured red. We are looking at it because we're playing a game devised by Henry: what do the different countries look like? I have started by saying that Italy looks like a boot and Sicily a ball about to be kicked. Henry describes India as being like the tool of the Stone Age man in my history book. I'm stuck for another simile. Henry points to Britain and Ireland, and says: 'A big brother reaching out to hold a baby brother.'

ACKNOWLEDGEMENTS ∫

POOR OLD MAN © 1995 Clare Boylan
SCARY MOVIES © 1995 Stephen Amidon
GEWÜRZTRAMINER © 1995 James Hamilton-Paterson
BERTRAM'S FUNERAL © 1995 Allan Massie
FALLING © 1994 Susan Johnson
THE MATRIARCH OF DEN AMSTEL © 1995 Roy Heath
DAMIAN'S DAY OUT © 1995 Christopher Hope
THE ICE WARRIOR © 1995 David Hartnett
HEROIN MAN © 1995 Tom Drury
THE PILLOW GOOSE © 1995 Jane Gardam
THE HERO © 1994 Joanna Trollope (a co-commission with
the *Daily Telegraph*)
NEGATIVES © 1994 E. Annie Proulx
THE HUMMING © 1995 Michèle Roberts
FINAL PAYMENTS © 1995 D.J. Taylor
AWAY FROM IT ALL © 1993 Frederic Raphael
(a co-commission with *Traveller* Magazine)
WAITING FOR MARILYN © 1995 Janice Galloway
SOME METAL BUILDINGS © 1995 Geoff Nicholson
SUMMER HOUSES © 1995 Philip Hensher
TO HER UNREADY BOYFRIEND © 1995 Helen Simpson
OUR GENIUS © 1995 Robert Cremins